IN SEARCH OF
CADIZ

KIM MACSYMIC

BREAKWATER BOOKS LTD.
100 Water Street • P.O. Box 2188
St. John's • NL • A1C 6E6
www.breakwaterbooks.com

Library and Archives Canada Cataloguing in Publication

Macsymic, Kim 1965-
      In Search of Cadiz / Kim Macsymic.

ISBN 1-55081-150-9

I. Title.

PS8625.S95I6 2006   jC813'.6   C2006-906565-9

The Canada Council | Le Conseil des Arts
for the Arts | du Canada

We acknowledge the financial support of
The Canada Council for the Arts for our publishing activities.

We acknowledge the support of the Government of Newfoundland
and Labrador, Department of Tourism, Culture and Recreation
for our publishing activities.

Canadä   We acknowledge the financial support of the Government of
    Canada through the Book Publishing Industry Development
    Program (BPIDP) for our publishing activities.

Printed in Canada.

For Kathleen and Liliane,
my grandmothers, who taught me the great strength of family.

First and foremost my thanks go out to Lindy Rideout who first conceived of the idea of a young man lost a sea, who did much of the research to give this novel its authentic voice, and who believed in me every step of the way. Thanks also to his wife, Lottie, who tolerated patiently our many emails, phone calls, and late night chats.

Thank you to Michelle Olivier, my first editor and dearest friend, who was both kind and constructive in her criticism, and to Sigmund Brouwer who took a rookie author under his seasoned wing to guide in the business of writing.

Thank you to Scott Ellison, Colin Hiscock and Dave Griffiths who went above and beyond in providing details for search and rescue missions and to Karen Ledrew-Day of The Beothuk Interpretive Centre in Boyd's Cove, NL.

Thank you to St. Peter's Grade Seven Class of 2004, my first audience, for providing feedback to reshape my first draft.

Thanks to my family and many friends who have encouraged and supported me through the long process.

Finally, thank you to my boys Connor and Keenan, and my husband Blair, for without love there is nothing.

1   TO SCHOOL

He stood in front of the bathroom mirror, blinking sleep from his eyes. He hated what he saw. He felt so average, so unexceptional. He wanted to be like the guys in the movies with their shiny hair, broad wry smiles, and six pack torsos. His eyes were an average brown, matched by average brown hair. His five foot six inch broad shouldered frame supported an average body, not husky, not wiry, not solid, just average. Brushing his average teeth, he thought of getting through another day at school, and it made him want to crawl back to bed. Grade ten had seemed full of promise last spring, but now it was the following May, and it had been nothing but one hassle after another. He consoled himself with the fact that it was Friday. He would sleep in tomorrow morning, perhaps until noon if his dad didn't drag him out to do yard work.

"Cadiz, get a move on b'y, you'll be ta missin' the bus."

It was his mother's usual morning song. It seemed that everyday of his life his mother had spent the morning nagging at him to get on that stupid bus. He splashed his face and raked a comb through his hair. He was happy to leave his reflection and walk back to his room. Sitting on the bed, putting on his socks, he glanced at the shelf above. Himself, his father, his brother, and his granddad, smiled down at him, frozen in a snapshot of a much happier time. He loved to think back on that fishing trip. Life was so simple then. Granddad looked so spry, Brian the poster-boy for success and Dad still the superman every boy believes his father to be. They had had things to talk about; lures, bait, technique, Granddad's bad jokes, mom's attempt at sandwiches, which ended up being masses of sweaty cheese and bread like wet papier mache. He pulled his jeans up loosely on his hips, then pulled a tattered sweatshirt over his head. He grabbed a crumpled bill, loose change and his trusted pocket knife, and thrust them into his pocket. He braced himself for the tension that had filled the kitchen as of late and walked downstairs.

His father sat with his head swallowed by the newspaper. His mother rummaged through cupboards, keeping busy, looking busy. She filled a brown bag with food no one wanted to eat, but which Cadiz hadn't the courage to turn down. He grabbed a glass from the cupboard and walked to the fridge. This was not the Brady Bunch. There was no "good morning," or "hello sleepyhead." His parents were never caught in a sweet start-the-day kiss. Instead there was just silence. A silence that filled the room, thick like a Newfoundland fog. Sometimes Cadiz felt like he would suffocate if made to sit there too long. He poured a glass of milk and drank it in one long drain as he leaned against the counter. He set the glass down, grabbed his lunch bag, and headed for the door.

"Put your glass in the sink," his mother ordered. With

a sigh, he walked back, lifted the glass, and with exaggerated purpose set it in the sink. He awaited a thank you, but it wasn't coming. He looked at his mother. Once a robust woman, she now looked deflated. Her upper arm jiggled as she wiped the counter, moved a cup from point A to point B, then turned to the table and began to wipe a stray crumb. She just didn't get it did she? She was always trying to save the world by tidying her house. Couldn't she see the world crumbling around her? Didn't she ever read the news? There were madmen with weapons of mass destruction, there were diseases, and people dying in earthquakes and avalanches, dying of starvation. It was unfair and there was nothing anyone could do about it. But his mother thought keeping a clean toilet would bring about world peace. He resumed his journey to the door, to get his shoes and back pack. He tossed in his lunch, grabbed his jacket and opened the door. In his head he heard "Bye son, have a nice day!," but it was a voice from a TV family, one he wasn't likely to hear in this house.

He slammed the door and trudged through the mud to the bus stop.

Newfoundland was turning warm in May and the sky was already a crisp blue. He longed for the days when the bus ride was a social occasion for happy chatter and good-natured teasing. As the bus pulled up he could see the group huddled at the back like some American fraternity. They all gave each other knowing looks, but Cadiz knew the secret they thought they were hiding. Ever since his troubles began, he knew they thought he was just that psycho kid who had lost it one day in Chemistry class.

He pushed that day from his thoughts, boarded the bus, and pretended not to notice their stares. He listened to the gears shifting, as the bus rumbled forward. The radio murmured in the background as it did every morning. Not loud enough to inform anyone of anything, the volume just enough to be annoying. The bus slowed for the Klassen kids. As they climbed on, Cadiz thought of his homework. How would he get out of it this time? Mr. Clark had told him no more excuses. He was sure to get a zero on the unfinished paragraph in his book bag. What a stupid assignment anyway. What was he supposed to learn by writing a composition explaining his favorite hobby? He knew what he liked and why he liked it. Why did it have to be analyzed, cheapened by words? Like he'd tell Clark anything personal or real anyway. The guy looked like Hitler with his half mustache and greased hair swooped off to one side. Cadiz didn't want anyone climbing into his head, especially not some misfit, no-life teacher. The landscape streamed by and after several stops and starts the school loomed ahead. Like most things in the area it was a nondescript building, a sandy brown rectangle surrounded by a grey moat of ashphalt. The bus jerked to a stop and Cadiz got up hurriedly to leave the bus before the back seat boys started their coughs of muffled jeers.

At the top of the stairs to the entrance way Cadiz hooked up with Rod. He and Rod Powers shared an English class, an attitude, and the love of a few cold beer. Rod's tall thin frame made him a walking squiggle: protruding forehead, bumpy nose, full lips, bobbing Adam's apple and a wiry body. With his checkered jacket and spitting-gap smile, he reminded Cadiz of an out of work court jester. Rod had the look, but neither the wit nor agility for slapstick. Cadiz found him a bit on the dense side, but at least he never gave a guy a bad time. They had been friends since fifth grade and when you needed to kick back and forget everything, Rod always showed you how.

Rod gave him a nod of greeting, "Hey, my son, you're lookin' a bit like a Monday mornin'. It's Friday, try to crack grin."

Cadiz sighed, "Ya, well, I'd be ta feelin' a whole lot better if it were 3:30. I don't have that damned paragraph ready for Clark. You?"

Rod's grin broadened a little, "Na, think it's important do ya?

"Hell no, but I bet he will."

The two boys sauntered the hallway to its mid-point. Rod veered left into his Art class while Cadiz went straight to Shop. Shop was one of the few classes he enjoyed. He loved working with his hands, especially with wood. He came from a long line of woodworkers. His great-grandfather had been a ship builder, as had grandfather and father too. His brother, Brian, had had a gift for wood. Brian had had a gift for everything. The three generations had always pointed the way. Cadiz couldn't remember a time when he had not known the sweet smell and comforting feel of freshly sanded wood. Consequently, Harris, the shop teacher was about the only teacher he could get along with. Harris seemed to understand that he didn't want to talk, only work with his hands. Harris gave him space, tools, and a little praise. That was all he really wanted. Not guys like Clark who poked around assigning writing or Ms. Simmons, the guidance counselor, who was always trying to get him to "open up." He liked her long legs and red hair, but that didn't mean she was going to get the scoop on his thoughts and dreams. Why did teachers always think they had some right to dig out a kid's feelings and try to read them, like some gypsy deciphering the future from pig guts! Shop, as always, went too quickly, and soon the bell shrilled for next class. English. The jig was up. Cadiz brushed sawdust from his jeans and had a fleeting thought of exiting the big garage door to the parking lot. Instead, he gave Mr. Harris a nod, and lumbered out the door to the hallway. Rod was waiting for him outside of Mr. Clark's class. Students bustled by and lockers slammed at irregular intervals along the corridor.

"Well," smirked Rod, "Lets say we stir up Adolf."

"No probs," Cadiz replied. "My homework is bound to get his eye to twitchin'."

They entered the room, found their regular seats at the back, and slid in as noncommittally as possible. As the bell shrilled once again, Mr. Clark entered. His characteristic frown was a little deeper set than usual. He tossed his books brusquely on the desk and passed a stony stare around the room. Cadiz knew this wasn't going to be a good Friday.

2   TENSION

With Cadiz off to school, Rose sat at the table, stirring sugar into coffee that had long passed its prime. She too was not what she had once been. She pulled her fingers through a tangle of salt and pepper hair. She had never seen it as her job to be fashionable or sophisticated. She was shaped by her environment, like a low lying blackberry bush, short and hardy, providing sustenance, clinging to what she knew. She had never seen herself as separate from what she did. She was a mother, a wife, and a Newfoundlander. In her youth she had thought herself fine, but never pretty; a solid woman who got the job done. Now her world seemed chaotic. She did not know the job, nor exactly how to tackle it. It all seemed beyond her, removed from her, like it was happening to someone else. John walked it breaking in on her thoughts.

"We should be thinkin' of gettin' rid of a few things." His voice had taken on a heaviness, like he was conserving each breath.

"Like what?" Rose asked, fearful that this would soon escalate. For the past few months every conversation was a dance on a tight rope.

"If we're to be movin', I don't want to be takin' everything we've ever found fit to buy. It's an opportunity to start fresh."

Rose's stomach tightened. She was not a pack rat. Anything she owned had value; if not practical, than sentimental. She could not imagine watching people pick through her life at some garage sale, could not imagine selling her memories for a few toonies.

"I can't say as I can think of much to be rid of." She tossed out the words like a kite, testing the direction of the wind.

"Hmm," John mumbled and made his way back to the livingroom. Rose sipped her coffee and reached for the newspaper laying abandoned on the table. She hated it when John began the weekend with the paper. It always left him feeling emasculated, as there was rarely good news for Newfoundland.

She let herself drift into nostalgia for bit. She had known John since elementary school, but she especially remembered the day he had made his interests known. They were in grade eleven, senior year back then. He had shyly invited her to the graduation dance. His height and square shoulders had grabbed her attention; his kind blue eyes and quiet strength had kept it. Being from different communities, she had been surprised to discover that his parents were short and square like she was. His mother's blue eyes had given her away. His father's stubborn streak was the legacy most apparent in his son. Despite her father-in-law's gruff exterior, she had found him quite charming. From the very beginning Rose had felt like she belonged to the family.

So much had changed over the years. The old ways had been run over, and with each new "progress" a little of the province had died. With it, perhaps, a little of the family had too. John's father had not found it in himself to embrace boats of fiberglass instead of wood, and had stubbornly passed his art on to her boys. Granddad had never forgiven John for his decision to leave a four generation business for the much less romantic world of trucking. Rose had admired John's practical nature and was more than willing to join him. But, with fish plants closing one-by-one, that life too had been stripped from them. There was nothing to do now but follow progress into the cities.

She didn't worry much about what she would find to do. There was always work for a woman who wasn't too proud to get her hands dirty, but she worried about John. He had lined up a job for the end of summer working construction in Yellowknife. His early years in his father's shop had made him handy. Granddad would be chuckling in his grave to know that fate had driven his son to a life with wood. Rose worried about Cadiz the most. She had questioned the wisdom of pulling Cadiz away from everything he knew, at a time when he seemed so unstable. In recent days she had barely spoken to her son. Even a greeting could sting when he chose not to reply. He had shut them out, and she had grown fearful of trying to get through to him. John had decided that a new beginning was what everyone needed. Predictably, Cadiz had disagreed with a vengeance.

John walked into the kitchen, pipe and tobacco in hand, and stopped to gaze out the window. He fumbled to fill the pipe, a recent habit. The window over the sink, looking out to sea, was Rose's favorite place in the whole house. It brought together all that she loved – her home, her family and the great beauty of the landscape.

As if reading her thoughts, John remarked, "It's a pretty view. I'll miss it." He turned to face her, "I knows you will too, Rose. I'm sorry life hasn't been all we expected. Look, I knows you don't want to leave, but I've found work and with the trouble Cadiz has been givin' us, I think it best. With dad gone now there's really not much keepin' us. With your family moved west there's not much difference if we're here or on the mainland."

They had discussed this before, and Rose had disagreed, but she could not find the energy to argue today. She simply nodded and crossed to the entrance. She straightened out the boots and shoes into neater rows and took the broom in hand. If she could not control where she was headed, she could at least make tidy where she was.

The hum of the class settled and Mr. Clark cleared his throat.

"I'm more than a little disappointed with the assignments from last week," he said as he moved to his briefcase and pulled out a tattered stack of paper. With a tight voice and a relaxed gait he moved through the aisles, handing back assignments.

"You'll have to be putting in a more serious effort if you hope to come out of grade ten with any kind of progress at all. How many of you have thoughts of a post secondary education?"

Cadiz saw several hands go up. He and Rod shared a look that said, "Whatever pal."

Mr. Clark continued, "I can't be the only one in here who cares about your education. You need to make that commitment for yourself." His words cut off just as he reached Cadiz's seat. Clark stared down at him. Cadiz gave him a brief look, then he let his eyes wander across the tiled floor.

"Well, Cadiz. I noticed I didn't get the privilege of reading your work. I do hope you have something brilliant to share with me today."

Cadiz shifted in his seat. "No, sir. Seems I forgot it at home."

Clark looked up at the class with a grin, "The old eyes are pretty good b'y, but I can't say they'd be strong enough that I can read your paper all the way from here."

A few students chuckled, but most bristled, knowing this could be the start of some unwelcome entertainment.

Clark continued, "If I can't see it then I can't mark it, and if I can't mark it, I guess I have to give you zero." He was again staring down at Cadiz, and an edge trimmed his voice. Cadiz still stared at the tiles. They began to undulate and swim before him, while Clark's voice took on an echo through his head.

"What's with you Cadiz? So much talent wasted, trapped in a body that doesn't give a crap…"

Cadiz had known Clark would ride his case, but in front of everyone? He could feel the heat rising in his face. Clark, thin-lipped and eyes slit, continued his tirade, but it was drowned by the rush of anger that had coursed through Cadiz, starting in his face and bolting like electricity through his limbs. Finally, his body came up out of his desk, knocking the table forward. Before he realized what had happened he was face to face with Clark, curses and saliva flying from his mouth. He released all of the morning's tension. He could not remember all the words, but he knew that he had told Clark to mind his own business, to butt out and get a life. With heavy, forceful steps Cadiz strode to the door, slamming it behind him. He heard a shatter of glass and knew the window in the door had broken, but he didn't look back. He would never look back. He would just keep moving forward, away from the school, away from the crappy towns that made up his life, away from his family, away from everything.

He slammed the outside door against the metal railing of the front entrance and as he hit the parking lot he began to run. He ran to the only place that gave him solace, the sea. There, on the shore, he slumped down exhausted. The rock at his feet supplied him with stones that he threw like ammo out into the water. With each stone came a question. Why? Why was Brian gone and not him? Why did Granddad have to be gone too? Why were his parents making him go to another no-place place? Why did Clark give a crap about what he did or didn't do? Why was life so unfair? Suddenly, he heard the crunch of an approach and looked quickly up behind him. Rod stared down with his crooked grin.

"Made quite a mess in there, son. Glass everywhere. Gave everyone a bit of a scare. Ol' Clark is probably scrapin' his shorts as we speak."

Cadiz wouldn't have thought it possible, but he felt a smile spread across his lips. Rod wasn't the brightest bulb, but he could always shed a little light.

Cadiz looked at the pattern of stones below his knees. "Ya,

I bet it didn't help me ditch the nickname Psycho, either." He looked up and out to sea. "Aren't you suppose to be in class young man, caring deeply about your education?" His voice dripped darkly with sarcasm.

Rod chuckled and settled in beside him. "Well, it I was really worried about my education, the first thing I'd have to do is transfer out of Hitler's class. I guess I'll be gettin' a little vacation anyway. I kind of flipped him the bird when I left." Now both boys were laughing. The thought of Clark, standing in a puddle of broken glass with a lost look on his face, made Cadiz feel suddenly warm, like he'd won a victory. Then a shadow crossed his thoughts again. "Do you ever think of taking off?"

His blunt question caught Rod off guard. "You mean like runnin' away?" Rod asked.

"Ya," Cadiz kept his gaze forward, "just gettin' on a bus and going west. Just going and going and never looking back. Maybe stopping when you can rest just like this, but on the Pacific edge."

"Sure," said Rod sorting through the gravel between his shoes, "but who has that kind of cash? I don't even have the money to get off The Rock, nevermind to the other side of the country."

Cadiz felt a bit of frustration at Rod's lack of vision, his inability to dream. "Okay, suppose you won the lottery, wouldn't it be great to just start fresh somewhere?"

"Can't even afford a ticket," giggled Rod.

Cadiz gave up and fell into silence. A few long minutes ticked by. Cadiz let his imagination run free. Not confined to this continent, he let it leap across the Atlantic, to a port in Spain. Before Cadiz's great-grandfather had turned to boat building, he had been a seaman. He had ended up in the pretty seaside city of Cadiz, Spain. It was there that he had received news of his impending fatherhood. He had hurried home to settle into family life and had named his son after the city. Half a century later, Cadiz had been named after his granddad. Cadiz Senior had always promised Cadiz Junior that they would go to Spain one day to visit the province and the city that had become part of their identities. Cadiz had seen glimpses of the port: directors of the movie "Die Another Day" had done some filming there because of its striking similarities to Cuba. A picture of the port, with its Moorish domes, hung in Granddad's stage. Cadiz had envisioned sitting in a cafe, drinking wine with his granddad; the two of them meeting beautiful Spanish women, Granddad entertaining them with his stories.

"So," Rod spoke, following Cadiz'z gaze across the bay and cutting off his escape, "what should we do with our free day?"

Suddenly Cadiz realized his parents might be getting a call. "Guess we should make the most of it. My folks will be freakin' when I get home. Whadda ya say we tromp over to your brother's place for a while? There's no phone, which should buy us some time."

Rod's brother Ernie was three years older, but he'd dropped out of school a year or two ago. He had a couple of low-life roommates and the typical grisly shack that went with the territory. Cadiz suspected that the guys earned a living selling dope, as there always seemed to be plenty of beer and groceries, loud music and company, but never anyone leaving for work. Although he wasn't crazy about the company, Cadiz liked hanging out at Ernie's. There were no adults nagging or hovering and, so long as Rod and he did a few dishes or took out the garbage, the guys never minded sharing a few beer.

Rod stood up, "Sounds like a plan."

Cadiz stood and brushed the grit from his jeans. The two boys walked up the beach in silence. As they hit the road that wound along the water's edge, Cadiz was struck by the calmness of the water. It was such a beautiful day and everything in his life was so ugly. They turned off Ferry Road and cut westward to Ernie's. Rod chattered on about some car he wanted to buy someday. Cadiz nodded and grunted at all the right times, but his thoughts were far away. They were with Granddad and Brian on a warm October afternoon, fishing.

3   CHICKEN & COURAGE

John looked out from his roof. With the house going up for sale it was time to clean the gutters and check the shingles. It was something he had been meaning to do and today was the perfect day. With hardly a breath of wind the bay was beautiful. From here he could see the expanse of the village, rather grey with the mud of spring and the rock not yet washed in the green of mosses. But the bare rock, open water and cloudless sky gave it a crisp strength. Each season had it's own beauty and he would miss it deeply. This was the home he had grown up in. The year his mother had died, the same year Cadiz was born, his father had built himself a small quarters above the stage. John had moved his family into his boyhood home, enjoying the link to his past. The boys shared the room that had been his. He felt that his mother would have been proud of the way he and Rose had kept the saltbox house, just as quaint and tidy as she had. He hoped he was making the right decision, dragging his family to the north. He had given Rose the choice, but in his heart, he knew it was he who had decided. Rose said she was reluctant for Cadiz's sake, but he knew her own heart was not in it. What could a man do? There were bills to pay and he felt he had run out of options in dealing with his son. Cadiz was a good boy, but he was making rash choices, not thinking clearly. He hoped that new surroundings would give Cadiz a new perspective and a new beginning. The past eight months had been hard on all of them.

A Bluejay perched on a popular branch just a few feet away. It made John think of his mother. She had loved the birds, and made an effort to keep them fed throughout the winter. It struck him that he had accepted his mother's death so much easier than his father's, and yet his mother's passing had been so much more difficult. Perhaps it was that very difficulty that had lightened the burden. After a two year battle with Cancer, her passing had seemed a blessing. He had been busy with his young family which also forced him to pull himself together and carry on. His father passing so suddenly meant no time for goodbyes and no time for apologies. He had to live with the regret now and it ate away at him, at first ferociously, then nudgingly, like wolves at an aging carcass. That day in October had been much like today. The sun had been shining and he had had big plans for working out doors with the boys.

He would put Brian here on the roof, while he and Cadiz worked on the yard. Granddad had other plans for his boys. It was in Cadiz Senior's bones that October meant fishing.

"The fesh will be at their fattest me lads," he would tell them.

John had argued with his father. How foolish it was to be out on the water, when any day the winds could be blowing in all kinds of harsh weather. He needed the boys at home. There may be no more weekends of such fine weather and the house needed batting down. It should have been done last month, but his father had had the boys busy in the shop, Brian finishing his kayak and Cadiz Jr. helping Granddad with odd jobs. In the end, however, Granddad had won. They had left to go fishing and John's last words to his father had been to tell him he was a stubborn old fool.

John rose with cracking knees. He was slipping on his work gloves when he heard Rose's voice calling his name. It was not like her to call him in unnecessarily, and so he made his way to the ladder. As he entered the house he was greeted by the robust smell of onions and garlic.

On the counter sat a bowl of cut up potatoes, and beside it the beginnings of a pile of sliced carrots. John's stomach gurgled at the thought of Rose's savory soup.

Rose sat at the table and the look on her face told John that he was not in for good news. He stood in the entrance and waited for her to speak.

"The school jus' phoned," she said. Her voice was tired. "Apparently Cadiz had some kind of run in wit' Ted Clark. Clark reprimanded him for some unfinished homework. They had words and Cadiz ran off. Rod went after him, so Clark figures they're together."

John's hunger was immediately replaced by a knot of anger. "Damned that boy! What is so hard about being fifteen? I asked him about homework las' noight and he told me it wasn't a problem. Call Rod's and tell him to get ta' hell home."

John stomped out the door and made his way back to the roof. Rose watched the door slam shut then walked heavily to the phone. She dialed, searching her mind for the right words. She loved her son deeply. How would she find the balance between tough love and kid gloves? The phone rang, again and again, then three more times. She felt both relieved and at a loss. She would not have to face another argument with her son nor a scolding she did not feel like giving. But she was not sure what to do next. Rose hung up the phone and turned her attention to the vegetables that littered the counter. She scooped up the carrots and dropped them into the pot bubbling on the stove. She added the bowl of potatoes and stirred, wishing her life could have come together as easily as her soup. At one time she believed it had. She turned the heat to simmer and made her way to the back porch. Putting on her jacket and boots, Rose went out to meet John on the roof.

As they entered Ernie's, Cadiz was met by the distinct and revolting stench of stale beer and lingering cigarette smoke. The drawn curtains, dark walls and faded brown shag left the house feeling more like a tomb than a home. Pop cans and beer bottles littered the floor and counter tops. A greasy box held the remains of chicken bones and a few cold, limp fries. Through the kitchen door that led to the living room Cadiz could see a lump of blankets on the couch. It may have been a sleeping body, but it was hard to tell. Rod walked over to the fridge, grabbed two pop and tossed one to Cadiz. The boys made their way to the living room where Rod flopped into a chair. Cadiz gingerly sat down on the carpet, reluctant to think about what might be living in the deep, dirty pile. The blankets on the couch rustled, confirming the presence of a body, likely one nursing a nasty hangover. Cadiz heard a toilet flush and then Ernie appeared in the door frame. He had serious bed head and his lily white belly hung over his baggy boxers.

"Hey Rodney, is it Saturday?," Ernie asked as he rearranged his boxers.

"No," Rod winked at Cadiz, then looked at his brother, "It's Friday, but me and Cadiz here are takin' an extended weekend."

Ernie made no comment, made his way to the couch and shook the lower half of the body buried there. A dirty blond head appeared and grunted, curling up its legs to leave room on the couch. Ernie flopped down and stretched his hairy legs out on the battered coffee table. A can tipped and rolled to the floor. Ernie ignored it, "What says you tells your brother a little more about this extended weekend."

Rod launched into the tale, embellishing at every opportunity. Cadiz sipped at his pop and stared at the wood paneling that covered the walls. Rod and Ernie's conversation became a mumbled blur as the counterfeit wood transported him to another time and place. The paneling reminded him of Granddad's shop. Cadiz had found it odd that his grandfather had chosen to cover the loft's walls a spurious version of his greatest passion.

Nonetheless the stage with its shop on the bottom and apartment loft above, had been a haven for Cadiz and his older brother. He and Brian had spent many hours there, hiding from their parent's list of chores and enjoying the equally demanding chores Granddad had given them. As they cut or sanded, swept or varnished, Granddad regaled them with tales, some true, some gilded, some that Cadiz suspected were out-right fiction. But the boys had listened to each one as if it were gospel. He especially liked Granddad's tales of survival. In one, he had told the boys how to boil water in a plastic bottle. That was a hard one to believe, so Granddad had shown them how. He also told them of the many ways to find fresh water, or to start a fire with little more than a stick and a boot lace.

Cadiz was tripped from his walk down memory lane by the sound of his name.

Rod was smirking at him, "Ya with us, son?"

"Sorry. What was that?" Cadiz asked.

"I'm getting' the growlies" said Rod, "What say we goes down to Margo's shack for somethin' ta eat?"

Ernie rose and walked across to the kitchen. He disappeared into the bedroom and came back with a handful of cash. "Picks me up some smokes and a frozen pizza."

The body under the blanket mumbled something and Ernie added, "Best get a couple of them pizzas."

Rod added his empty pop can to the collection on the coffee table and took the bills from his brother, stuffing them into his pocket. He and Cadiz made their way to the door and stepped outside. After the gloom of the house, the sun felt brilliant. The sky was an intense blue. The asphalt road continued eastward, then wound south to Margo's. Every village had a place like Margo's; a convenience store with an eclectic assortment of merchandise.

Cadiz tossed his can into a large recycle barrel outside the store. When he walked in he smelled a mixture of greasy chicken, chocolate, and dust. The first few racks lured children with row upon row of gum, chocolate bars and nickel candy. Past that were shelves where chips and pie fillings sat next to laxatives and rubber gloves. An entire shelf was dedicated to Newfoundland's own Purity products, where rows of silhouette caribou arched skyward. Along the left wall, coolers displayed frozen goods, ice and soft drinks. The back wall housed a beer cooler on the left. On the right Margo dished out her not-so-famous chicken and fries. Through the right wall widow the sun beamed in on faded magazines, motor oil, and car fresheners. Cadiz could see the dust floating in the sunbeams, defying gravity as it hovered there.

The boys made their way to the coolers and found the pizzas. The ice encrusted around the edges told Cadiz that they were not one of Margo's more recent purchases. He reached into his pocket and found a five, two toonies and a bit of silver. The sign on the back wall, above the food window, indicated that he would have enough for one of Margo's dinners.

"I'm optin' for chicken," he told Rod.

"I'm opting for whatever me brother's buyin," replied Rod.

Rod grabbed two pizza's, set them on the counter, then went to settle in at the magazine rack. Cadiz walked over to the back wall where Margo leaned through the window.

"Well, Cadiz, me boy. How are ya?," she asked.

"Jus' fine," said Cadiz, "but I'd be a whole lot better with some of your *fine chicken*." Cadiz noted the white lie. Fine chicken? He could be charming when he wanted to be. Grease soaked, under-spiced chicken would not be his first choice, but it beat freezer burned pizza or hunger for that matter.

"I'll have a dinner pack."

Margo about faced and headed for the frier. Cadiz joined Rod at the magazines to await his fine chicken. The boys thumbed through pages of cars they would likely never own, girls they would likely never meet and issues they would likely never face.

"Hey Cadiz, want to take a survey to rate your sex life?," Rod's smile was broad as he held up a page of a man and woman frolicking through a Caribbean Sea with a host of questions at their feet.

"Think I'll pass there stud muffin. But you go right ahead." Cadiz feigned seriousness for a second, then matched Rod's smile.

"Na too depressing to see the big fat zero at the end," replied Rod.

A thought suddenly occurred to Cadiz. On the way into the store he had noticed the pay phone, outside, just to the right of the door. It occurred to him that he should phone home. Surely they would have heard from the school by now. He imagined his mom cleaning madly as his dad paced the floor. Would it be better to phone and face the music from a distance, or should he prolong the agony and face them later tonight?

"Hey Rod, think we could crash at Ernie's tonight?" he asked.

Rod looked up from a page of an Auto Trader and nodded affirmatively. Cadiz set down the magazine he'd been skimming and headed for the phone.

"Be right back," he called over his shoulder. He'd made a plan. He would face the music from a distance, then hope they would let him stay at Rod's. This would give them time to cool off and they would be grateful he had called them instead of making them hunt him down. The worst that could happen is they would demand he head home. He would have to make an excuse to miss the bus. He just wasn't ready to face the frat boys again today. He dug a quarter from his jeans and reached for the phone. He inhaled deeply as he punched in the numbers, then exhaled as it began to ring.

Rose climbed the ladder to the roof. There she found John laying flat on his stomach clutching a handful of debris from the gutters. He tossed the mess of mud and rotted leaves from his hands and she watched it splatt against the ground. A little trail below followed his progress along the eves. He looked up at her as she mounted the roof.

"Well, what's the word?" he asked.

"There's no answer at the Powers," she sighed. "Maybe I should drive in and look for him."

John began a push up, then swiveled into a sitting position. He too sighed and looked down at nothing in particular. He shook his head. "I don't know." He had felt this sense of indecision a lot lately. "Maybe we should let him cool off for a bit. I just don't know." He turned to Rose, awaiting her advice. He could see the concern in her eyes, that awful strain she had come to wear daily, the look that showed fear and love, heartbreak and hope, all at the same time.

"I suppose it wouldn't hurt to wait a bit," she suggested. "He and Rod are probably wandering around somewhere deciding what to do." Rose brushed a stray hair from her eyes and continued, "But let's not wait too long. I'll feel better when I know 'is state of mind."

She sat next to her husband and the two looked out

over the village to the water. A sea gull swooped off in the distance, seemingly surfing the sky. John began to chuckle, "Do you remember the day Brian taught Cadiz how to work a snare with a piece of twine?"

Rose smiled too. Brian had only been about thirteen then, Cadiz about nine. The boys had spent all afternoon trying to snare a seagull that had been plaguing the garbage. John went on, "Cadiz finally caught that silly bird, but he was so startled he let go of the twine. I still remember him chasing after that damned bird, with the string hangin' down like a runaway kite." John was belly laughing now. Rose joined him. It had been quite the sight, made even funnier watching Brian roll across the lawn, laughing so hard he couldn't sit up. It felt so good to laugh and to remember; to remember without the weight of the loss bearing it down.

"Did he ever catch it?," Rose asked as her laughter subsided.

John shook his head. "No, and I'd like to have seen the look on that seagull's family when he flew in all a tangle. Pop's been drinkin' and flyin' again mama..." John continued to chuckle. Rose noted that it had been awhile since she'd heard such a thing from John. He had a habit of picturing animals with wives and kids, complete with Chesterfields, TVs and remote controls. Once a polar bear had rummaged through Granddad's stage, down by the beach, and upset a can of red paint. The prints indicated that the bear must have been pretty painted up before he moved on. John had commented then, "Bad enough for a man to come home with lipstick on his collar – imagine him showing up with it all over his body. Bet ol' mama bear has him sleeping on the couch tonight!" The boys, young then, had had giggle fits for the rest of that evening, picturing polar bears driving cars, grocery shopping and using the toilet. Rose recalled how close the boys had always been. Brian had always been protective of his baby brother and Cadiz had revered his older brother as an all knowing sage.

The stillness of the late morning sun was suddenly interrupted by a shrill ring. Rose leapt to her feet and hustled down the ladder. If she hurried she could catch the phone on the third or forth ring. As her feet hit the ground she heard ring number two. Ring number three screamed just as she opened the back door. She lifted the receiver just as the forth ring began. "Hello?" she panted.

"Hi, Mom." Cadiz's voice was hesitant and small, like when he was a little boy.

4   THE LAST ANCHOR

"Cadiz, where are you?" Rose could feel her heart thumping madly in her chest. Questions flooded her thoughts. Should she be firm or gentle? Would this be a fight or a moment to be close? Was he angry? "Are you OK? I spoke with Ms. Simmons and she told me about you and Mr. Clark. What happened?" The words raced over her tongue before she even realized it.

"Um, well…" Cadiz hesitated trying to find the right words. "Mom? I'm really sorry. I know I should have had my work done. I just got mad when he started freakin' on me in front of everyone. I'm sorry Mom. I'm with Rod right now. I had to leave the school, just to calm down." He awaited a response, testing the waters to see if he dared to ask to stay with Rod.

"Cadiz, we have to go for a meetin' at the school on Monday mornin'. There'll be a suspension, but they wants to speak to me and your dad." Rose tried to measure her tone, firm, but kind. "I think it's best that you get home now, so that we can discuss this."

"Um…" Cadiz summoned up his reserves. "Do you think I could spend the weekend wit' Rod and meet you at the school Monday?"

Rose was incredulous, "Cadiz, this is serious! You can't just go gallivantin' around all weekend!" Rose strode quickly to her simmering soup and raised the lid.

"Mom, I know it's serious. I just need some time to think, you know? I know I made a mistake and I'll apologize to Mr. Clark."

"We still need to discuss this Cadiz. It's more than just what's happened at school. We need to talk, as a family." Rose stirred the soup, feeling her resolve dissolve with the salt and spices.

"Could I at least have a couple days? Mrs. Powers could drive me home Sunday. We could talk after supper. Please Mom?" Cadiz's voice pleaded and it reminded Rose of when he's been a little boy, asking to stay up just a little longer, or to keep a stray kitten.

Rose sighed trying to decide what was best. She hated to admit it to herself, but the thought of avoiding the discussion for a couple of days was appealing. Her mind darted from one option to another, like a crazed humming-bird. For Cadiz the pause was an era.

"Mom?"

"Alright Cadiz," she caved, "but you be home Sunday. I don't want to walk into that school Monday without all the details. You best be thinking 'bout how you're goin' to replace that broken window. Am I clear?" She tried to sound strong, but she knew she had already given in more than she should have.

"Thanks Mom," Cadiz replied with sudden cheer in his voice. "I promise. I'll see you Sunday." Cadiz hesitated then.

He wanted to say "I love you," but the words just didn't come. It wasn't the style in his house, even though he could make it happen. Instead he said "Thanks" again and they both gave a perfunctory "Bye."

Cadiz hung up the phone and walked back into Margo's. She was at the counter handing Ernie's cigarettes and change to Rod. Cadiz noted his bag of chicken on the counter and made his way to the candy rack. He picked out a roll of Butter Rum Lifesavers, a craving he had inherited from his dad. He placed them next to the chicken and began digging for his cash. He and Margo exchanged a polite smile, as he took his change, then he and Rod made their way outside. Cadiz tore open the end of the Lifesavers and offered one to Rod.

"Naw, think I'll steal one of Ernie's sticks," Rod said as he unwrapped the cigarettes.

"Them things will kill ya," Cadiz commented as he popped a Lifesaver into his mouth.

The two boys chatted along the sun drenched road, enjoying the first heat of spring. The road had the wet dirt smell that accompanied May and a hint of salt blew east off the water. "Told my mom I'd be with you all weekend. Think your mom can drive me home Sunday?" Cadiz asked.

"Ya, I guess," replied Rod, "We"ll have to swing by there some time and find out her plans."

Rod's mom was a single parent. His dad had gone off to find work when Rod was in grade three. By grade five they were hearing from him less and less. By grade seven he had all but disappeared, along with any financial support. Rod had seemed to take it in stride, but the fact that he never spoke of it made Cadiz believe it had cut deeper than he let on. Cadiz also wondered if it was what had prompted Ernie to quit school so early and start out on his own. Mrs. Powers worked two jobs, which had pretty much left the boys on their own most of the time anyway.

Cadiz's thoughts returned to their weekend plans. "If it's a problem I'm sure one of my parents can drive in and get me."

"I can't believe they didn't make you head home," said Rod.

"Ya, I'm a bit surprised about that meself, but I figures they don't want a heavy discussion any more than I do." Cadiz's thoughts turned to the many disagreements they'd had as of late. Why was that, he wondered? After the accident no one really said much of anything. Then later, there had been the blow up at school. Then his parent's decision to move. Now the blow up with Clark. It just seemed to be spiraling and he wasn't sure if he could ever reign it in again. At times he wanted to, at other times he just didn't care. He loved the thought of just running from it all, which made his anger at moving to Yellowknife all the more ironic.

As they turned into Ernie's yard, Cadiz had an overwhelming aversion to re-entering the gloom. "Wanna eat out here?," he asked Rod.

"Hmmm" Rod dragged on the cigarette. "Jus' let me get them pizzas goin'."

Rod disappeared into the house, while Cadiz dug into the bag and began to eat.

Rose had called John in for lunch and set the table. As he washed up, she approached him with her news, as nonchalant as possible.

"Cadiz called. He's okay – just needs a little time. I told him to be sure to be home Sunday night, so we could have a good talk before the meetin' Monday. I think Ellie's gonna drive him home."

John stopped drying his hands and turned to face her. "What?! Rose, the boy is on the verge of bein' kicked outta school and you're let him wander about Nell's Cove all weekend? He should be here, and doin' hard labour at that! Land sakes woman."

Rose felt her cheeks flush. She was angry with his apparent condescension, but she herself wasn't sure why. Was it because she had every right to make a decision as a parent, or was it because she felt her husband was right, and she hadn't had the strength to do it? "You said yourself, he might need time to calm down."

"Well yes, time meanin' a few hours, not the entire weekend." He helped himself to a bowl of soup and pulled up to the table. He pulled his chair in roughly and shook the salt and pepper much too hard."

Rose filled her bowl and joined him at the table. Although they ate side by side, a chasm stretched out between them. In its vastness and silence Rose contemplated how they had arrived *here*. Why were things falling apart *now*? She remembered the first few days after the funerals. There had been so much to do and it had deferred the pain. They had been called to the school shortly after. Cadiz's Chemistry teacher had said Cadiz had threatened her with a knife. When all was said and done, it turned out that the mainland newcomer hadn't realized that in

Newfoundland pocket knives are common. Everyone whittles. She had demanded Cadiz's knife, a knife that his Granddad had given him for his eighth birthday. Cadiz had tried to show her the inscription on the blade. She had mistook his gesture as threatening. So had his classmates who has since burdened him with the label "Psycho." Cadiz had become introverted then, keeping his thoughts and feelings to himself. He had begun sessions with Ms. Simmons, but with little change to his demeanor. Winter had blown in and all had gone cold and quiet. Like Novocain on a bad tooth, it had only numbed him, healing nothing. Now spring had come. The time when Brian should be returning from college. The time when Granddad should be preparing his boat and gear. Just as the snow melts, revealing the rot of fall, the old pain was revealed afresh. John rose, set his bowl in the sink, mumbled a thank you and went back outside.

As Cadiz ate the last of his fries, Rod came out the door with his first piece of pizza. It was nice sitting in the sun enjoying an ill gained day off. Cadiz had to keep pushing troublesome thoughts away. What was Ms. Simmons going to say to his parents? Would Mr. Clark accept an apology? Would his parents support him in the meeting or would the adults all take one side and leave him in a great open space alone? What about Yellowknife? Would he ever fit in? Would he find friends or be the Newfie outsider? What would school be like? Could he enjoy IA Shop there? He sighed and stretched out on a piece of plywood laying dried and cracked in the grass. Rod munched away, apparently oblivious of the trouble they had gotten into that morning.

Ernie appeared at the door and spoke to them through the screen. "You boys wanna join the party?" he asked.

Rod swallowed his mouthful of greasy cheese and pepperoni. "Wha's up?"

"Greg finally got off the couch and rolled us a 'J'." Time you two got to experience the real world," he smiled coyly.

Rod looked at Cadiz. Cadiz looked back. Rod jumped up and went into the house. Cadiz hesitated then followed. The doleful house seemed to swallow them like a humpback feeding on krill, and a claustrophobia clutched at Cadiz, making him tense. Ernie and Greg sat side by side on the couch, a bag of green powdery leaves lay open on the coffee table. Cadiz knew from his DARE class what it was. He had seen glimpses of it at school in the boys' washroom as guys exchanged bags for cash, and he had known since sixth grade that this was not a place he was willing to go. Rod looked like an excited, but frightened, puppy curled up at the legs of the coffee table. Cadiz searched his mind for an out. Where did he have to be or what did he need to do that would suddenly call him away from here? He could think of no excuse. The boys lit the joint and began to pass it around. Rod looked at Cadiz and grinned, but Cadiz could not bring himself to smile in return. Instead he shook his head, hoping Rod would catch his meaning.

Rod's eyebrows came together, "Whats samatter?" he asked.

Now all three boys were looking at Cadiz.

Cadiz stammered, "Sorry guys, jus' not my thing." He

tried to sound casual, but he could hear the tension in his voice. Rod and Ernie shared a look and all three boys broke into ear to ear smiles.

"Come on, its a good time. Give it a try," Greg chuckled.

Rod sat up closer to the table. "I've been mighty curious about this. Come on Cadiz, might as well try it wit' the brother than look like a couple a losers tryin' it wit' girls around or somethin', lookin' foolish."

Cadiz wanted to tell him he looked foolish enough already, like a salivating dog waiting for a poison bone, but instead he turned and walked outside. He sat on the piece of plywood, waiting for the boys to be finished.

This would make it easier he thought. If Rod was going to start this stupidity, leaving for Yellowknife would be easier. He began to wonder why or how he and Rod had ever ended up pals in the first place. Rod was about as deep as a inverted frisbee and not nearly as quick. They shared few things in common, but Rod had been the only one who had befriended him when things began to spin. He had been one of the few to give him space after the accident. So many people had tried to be helpful with their stupid condolences and empty sentiments about not blaming himself. What did they know?! Rod was like a pet, mute and there. But Rod was changing. His once endearing nonchalance now seemed mindless, his offhand manner, reckless. *Great*, Cadiz thought with bitterness, *the one person in my life I could relax with and now that's gone too!*

A silhouette crossed the screen door and Cadiz looked closer. Rod walked, squinting into the sunlight. His goofy grin was more askew than usual and Cadiz did not like the shadow that hooded his eyes.

"Man, you're missin' a good time b'y." Rod said. "I feel great, like I could run a marathon."

"Ya, but you couldn't, could you?" Cadiz's voice was edgy. "Wonder how you'll feel in a few hours?" He was staring at his friend like he'd never really looked at him before.

"Gad, Cadiz. You gotta loighten up. What's your big problem anyway?" Rod asked staring down from the top step.

"No problem" Cadiz snapped, "I jus' don't go for the pothead routine."

"Ya, well at least I knows who I am," Rod replied with contempt.

"What's that suppose to mean?" Cadiz felt a raging dog begin to run through his chest.

"It's been eight months, Cadiz, don't you think you should let things go? One minute you're mister tough guy who's gonna run off, the next minute your phonin' your mommy to see if you can stay out to play. Make up your mind b'y."

Cadiz could feel the harsh words bubbling up from his throat. He tried to swallow them, but out they came. "Make up my mind to what, be a loser like you and Ernie?"

Cadiz saw the tendons tighten in Rod's neck, but in his anger, he pushed further. "What would you know about letting things go. Your dad walks out and you don't even give a crap."

Suddenly Rod sprang from the steps, pouncing on Cadiz and knocking him flat against the plywood. Rod got one good swing at Cadiz's jaw before Cadiz twisted his body, kicking his legs around Rod's midriff and pulling himself on top. Brian's wrestling lessons were paying off. He straddled Rod, holding his right forearm tight against Rod's neck, his legs pinning Rod's arms. Rod was kicking his legs, but to no real use. Cadiz held his left fist at his shoulder, ready to strike at Rod's face, when suddenly Ernie was shouting from the doorway. He and Greg grabbed at Cadiz and pulled him off. Rod sputtered, clutching at his neck. Cadiz didn't resist the two boys, and they soon let him go. He could hear their questions, and Rod coughing, but he didn't have the will to respond. He turned and walked away. Away from the scene and the only real friend he had left.

5   AT SEA

*C*adiz made his way to the main road that snaked its way north along the coast to home. His heart had slowed and the wild dog that had been raging inside him was resting, but alert. A faint breeze was picking up. Cadiz liked the smells it brought with it; the metallic scent of rock, the salt water, the cool of May. Out beyond the bay he could see a large floe, moving like a great glass barge. As he made his way well out of the village, before the coast turned east toward Goose Neck Ridge, he veered west. This took him to the cut line and would take considerable time off his journey home. A canopy of evergreens filtered the sun and Cadiz could feel the temperature drop. Spring may have arrived, but winter still whispered here. He picked up his pace and occupied himself with the surroundings. Last fall's Labrador Tea leaves littered the forest floor. It was a musky tea his mom had always enjoyed making on camping trips. With honey, it was the best thing for washing down Jiffy Pop made on the open fire. He had loved to watch the foil unfurl as it popped and sent out hot wisps of steam. The low bush partridge berries looked scraggly, awaiting much more sunshine to produce. Traces of droppings told him he might meet a moose, and the more human looking pile told him to be aware that he was in bear country.

The sun moved west as Cadiz made his way north to home. The cut line eventually opened on to the main highway. The first fifteen minutes provided no traffic, then with luck, the first to approach was a semi. Cadiz stuck out his thumb, blushing inside at the cliché feeling. The air brakes sounded and Cadiz jogged to meet the truck. The bearded, heavyset driver was headed to a crab plant further north, then moving south, off the island.

"Make ya a deal young fella," he had offered. "You help me find the plant and I'll drop you to your doorstep."

"Deal," said Cadiz. He had a fleeting thought of riding along, going wherever the man and his truck would take him. They made the usual small talk of strangers until they reached the plant. Cadiz knew it well, as his mother had once worked there. As the trucker backed in his trailer, Cadiz was overcome by the distinct smell of fish. Granddad had always chuckled at Cadiz Junior's repulsion to the smell of raw fish. How many generations had lived off the sea? And it made Cadiz as queasy as a landlubber. He slouched down in the seat and closed his eyes. Shortly, the trucker returned and the two resumed their small talk. It was refreshing to have a conversation with someone who didn't know his past. Soon they were approaching the turn off to the town. Cadiz's fantasies of running away had been replaced by the logic of empty pockets.

"This is fine," said Cadiz. "I wouldn't mind a bit of fresh air." He didn't want to offend his good Samaritan, but with a tail wind he had been forced to smell crab all the way home. He watched the truck chug off down the highway and he began the last few kilometers home.

As he approached the town, he felt exhausted. The thought of sleep was delicious. If he returned home, his parents would pepper him with questions and that thought made him even more weary. Along the water's edge he noted Granddad's stage. He hadn't been there since shortly after the funeral. He had helped his parents clean out the fridge, cupboards and a few other things, but he had not been back since. Being at Granddad's had churned up too much heartache, so he had avoided it. As far as he knew, his parents had rarely been there either. He felt compelled now to go there. Perhaps it was instinct. Spring always meant time in the shop, preparing for boating and fishing. He needed a connection to Granddad and Brian. He was missing them more lately. Odd that his longing for them had swelled as of late. He felt in his pocket for Granddad's knife. He had carried it with him everywhere since he was eight years old. It felt warm in his hand, reassuring.

He made his way down the rocky drop that led to the stage with its loft apartment above. Grandad had kept it in the traditional ochre colour. It was the last on the point, its east and south walls facing the sea. At the base of the slope, the west wall held the door, neatly trimmed in white. There he was met by a large padlock which must have been put there by his father after they had cleaned up the place. Cadiz skirted the building, looking for an in. The two large doors on the east side were locked from the inside. The stage's stilts made the south windows much too high for entry. On the north side of the building he found a window he could reach. He used his knife to jimmy it open a crack, then slid the blade along the latch until it released. Cadiz braced himself against the building and pushed upward. He had to rock the dried wood frame back and forth, until it finally slid up and gave him his opening. He climbed into the window which led to a countertop in Granddad's shop. The fine sawdust tickled his nose and swirled up into his eyes. He slid his belly along the counter, swung his legs inside and dropped to the floor. Brushing the sawdust from his chest and thighs, he began to look around. As his eyes adjusted to the dim light he could see the little world his Granddad had to leave behind. Sawhorses stood sentinel in the center of the room, and overhead beams cradled several sizes and lengths of wood. The east wall faced the water, with its large doors for hauling the boats out to sea. The south wall was lined with cupboards, which held Granddad's many tools, paints, and trade secrets.

Cadiz wanted to explore, but the long walk and the stuffy shop made his eyes heavy. He made his way up the stairs along the west wall, over the padlocked entrance. He opened the door to the loft and was struck with how nothing had changed. Of course, why would it have? No one came here. It was just as Granddad had left it, just as Cadiz and his parents had left it. The only tell tale sign of desertion was the dust, settled like a shroud over everything, and the fridge, gaping open, awaiting food like a hungry beast. The curtains were pulled and shards of light reflected on the dust Cadiz had stirred with his entrance. A potbelly stove, long gone cold, gave Cadiz a chill. He made his way to Granddad's bedroom and curled up on the bed. Pulling the blanket over him, Cadiz was overcome by the scent of Granddad's pipe. He closed his eyes and felt warm tears brim them. He left the tears, his arms seeming too heavy to move. Sleep came quickly, a welcome escape. But its comfort would be only temporary.

It was a warm October day. Cadiz knew his dad did not approve of their fishing trip, but he was excited all the same. A day on the water with Granddad was always an adventure. He had been in charge of toting supplies down to the old skiff while Brian organized the gear and Granddad packed a lunch. Granddad was famous for his lunches. Plenty of smoked fish, boiled eggs, biscuits and root beer. Not a fruit or vegetable to be found, and that's just the way they all liked it!

The day was crisp, the sun warm. Fluffy white clouds, suspended from a rich blue sky, reflected in the gently rippled Atlantic. They had fished all morning, then broke for lunch on Spirit Island. Granddad had shown them how to use moss as a bandage when Cadiz had nicked his palm while whittling. After lunch they had hit a few more good fishing grounds at the edge of the banks where upwelling made the fish more plentiful. Before long the wind had come up, gaining momentum like a boulder down a hill. Granddad looked out at the southern sky. He made Brian read the grey clouds there. Brian had done well and Cadiz had listened attentively, knowing the lesson was to teach him as much as it was to test Brian. Granddad had decided it was best they pack up and begin heading in. The clouds looked ominous, making it hard to believe that they had looked like the home of angels just a few hours before.

Brian began to pack the cooler and tidy the boat, while Granddad barked the orders like the captain that he was.

"Cadiz, me b'y, git that gaff in. Its time to head'er back. The rain'll be here in no time."

Cadiz tried to steady his feet at the rear port corner, but it was difficult with the long length of rope coiled there and the waves teetering the boat. He gripped the dirty hemp and began to raise the anchor. The rope bit into his cut palm and he let go. The anchor went hurling back to the ocean floor, and as it did, caught his legs. Off balance, Cadiz suddenly pitched forward and toppled into the icy water. Without warning, he had cried out, releasing precious air. He gulped and flailed stirring salt water into his mouth and eyes. The rope entangled his legs like an angry sea snake. Everything he'd been taught about falling overboard left him, washed away by animal panic. He heard voices and felt Brian in the water beside him, cutting the line. Granddad was pulling him inside the boat. He could not feel his fingers as he pulled his hands to his face, coughing the cold water out of his lungs. Suddenly Granddad was shouting over the port side. Cadiz leapt up to see. Brian was treading water, but an invisible force was pulling him under.

"He's caught in the damned gaff," he heard his Granddad mumble. Granddad pushed him aside and made his way to the steering wheel. He turned over the engine, cranked the wheel and circled Brian.

"Cadiz, reach him a paddle. Quick, b'y!" Granddad shouted.

Cadiz fumbled with the paddle, his numb fingers useless. He reached it out to his brother. Brian snatched it hard and the tug bolted the paddle from Cadiz's hands.

"Come grab the wheel!" Granddad called out over his shoulder. "Keep 'er as she is " he told Cadiz, as he handed over the steering.

Granddad swung out a second paddle, but it was too

late. Brain was gone, pulled down by twenty kilos of iron, swallowed by a hungry sea that had claimed so many Newfoundlanders before him.

Granddad reached over and killed the engine. Cadiz scurried out of the way and over to gaze into the water. What had just happened? He began to shout Brain's name, searching the water for a sign of him. He turned to find assurance from Granddad. What he saw made his hot panic turn to ice. Granddad was slumped forward, clutching the radio mouthpiece to his chest.

Cadiz ran to him, "Granddad, what is it?"

"It's me heart b'y," he whispered. "Start up the boat and get us home. You knows the way. Radio the Coas' Guard."

The world slowed to half speed as Cadiz's mind tried to make sense of the madness.

"What about Brian? Granddad, we can't just go!" Cadiz's voice was beginning to break. Hot tears had sprung on to his face. He was beginning to shout the words. "Brian! God, no!" The world swirled around him as he edged around the rim of the skiff searching for his brother. The rain began, falling in thick heavy droplets.

"Now, Cadiz, or we'll all die." Granddad's voice was faint, but it broke in and gripped Cadiz's terror. The purple in his own fingers told him he was freezing. Granddad's pale and slick face told Cadiz they needed a doctor. He could not save Brian, but he would save his Granddad. He helped him to the passenger seat, and wrapped a blanket around him. He grabbed Brian's jacket, abandoned on the deck, wrapped it around himself and started the engine. Granddad was right. He did know the way. He held a steady course, cutting through the waves and rain, noting the landmarks that were pointing them homeward. He had alerted the Guard and they would meet them at the dock with the paramedics. Granddad would be okay.

At the dock the medics had swept Granddad away. Cadiz had been whisked away in a separate ambulance, his mother at his side, his dad following close behind in the truck. The comfort of the hospital bed had been overwhelming. He could not remember ever being so warm or so tired. When he awoke he was startled. He had expected to find a nurse, the smell of antiseptic, tubes running out his hands. Instead there was a dusty gloom. He smelled Granddad's pipe.

It all came tumbling back. He was in Granddad's loft. Granddad was not okay. He had died in the ambulance all those months ago. The pain gripped him like it was yesterday. Great sobs surged his body and he cried hard and long. He screamed at the still room and slapped at the pillows, "Why? Why? Why?" Why had he been so careless to fall in the sea? Why had he panicked, forcing his brother to jump to his rescue? Why had he been spared instead of Brian? Why had he wasted precious moments that could have saved his Granddad? The photos on the walls and figurines on the bureaus offered no reply, sitting mute to the questions that tormented him. The tears continued until the rabid dog inside him had run its course.

Cadiz went from the bed to the bathroom. He longed to wash the sorrow from his heart and eyes, but the tap echoed up a faint noise and no water. The utilities had been cut off. He wandered the loft looking at the many pictures on the walls and shelves; aunts, uncles, cousins, a grandmother he knew only through stories, his parents' wedding, he and Brian at various ages, and a black and white photo of a Spanish port he would never visit with his Granddad.

He made his way back down to the shop. As he descended the stairs he saw something under the counter. He hadn't noticed it earlier, as he had slid in and hadn't looked back. Hiding under the counter, was Brian's kayak. Cadiz crouched and ran his hand along its starboard side. His hand made a trail through the dust and its shiny surface peeked through. At the hull he could make out the calligraphy – "Seaknife." Brian had come up with the name and had hoped she would live up to it, cutting smoothly through the water.

Cadiz had not been out to sea since that horrible day it had stolen his brother. It was time. He gently slide the boat onto the saw horses. She was a fine specimen. It was his fault Brian had never been able to launch her. Cadiz would take her now. He would take her out to meet her maker, find the spot Brian had gone down and float there a while. He checked his watch; 4:13 p.m. He checked out the window. The sky had clouded a little and the breeze had turned the sea to a liquid, rippling steel. It would be easy to launch her and the lengthening days meant he could be back in plenty of time before dark.

He unlatched one of the large doors and pushed it out on squeaking hinges. The door swung out and a little gust stirred the shop to life again. He slid a paddle into the Seaknife and swung the kayak up over his head to rest on his back and the nape of his neck. He walked several meters to the end of the wharf that extended from the building, out into the harbour, and set the kayak down. Cadiz returned to the shop and slipped on a slight jacket from those that hung by the door, ignoring the nets, spray skirts, and life jackets beside them. He closed the door, and went to set the kayak in the moving tide.

Stepping gently into the cockpit, he pushed her out to sea. True to her name she cut the water evenly and silent. The angry dog that had hounded his insides all day seemed to disappear. The movement of the boat and the hush of the wind calmed him. He had missed the feel of the paddle, the way its motion massaged away all the tightness and anxieties of life. He paddled east out of the harbor, rounding Hummock Point to travel north: north out to sea, north to the rich fishing grounds, north to introduce *The Lady Seaknife* to his brother.

The many islands peppered the coastline, some merely large boulders poking their heads through the surface, some large enough to deceive one into believing they were endless. Large motor craft could only skirt the outer edge or opt for open water. Cadiz enjoyed the agility and freedom of the kayak. It sliced through the many channels, snaking in and out of the narrow ones with ease, then bobbing along like a controlled buoy when Cadiz occasionally steered through the wider ones or entered open water. In the narrow passages, Cadiz could imagine he was the only life in a sliver of silver amid vast rock. In the open, he imagined great sea creatures sliding silently beneath the boat. The channels, while offering some protection from the wind, could be treacherous with the eddies that swirled and curled in on themselves. Cadiz maneuvered the little craft with confidence, his muscles welcoming the exertion. *If only I could navigate so smoothly through life*, he thought. Out here it was easy to believe life could be simple; the cool breeze, the hypnotic glint of the water, the wide sky fringed by clouds like distant grey mountains made daily troubles seem distant and small.

His eyes drifted from the seagulls circling overhead to the thoughts circling his mind. It had been an eventful day. He had alienated everyone. He wanted the chaos in his life to stop, but it seemed to swirl with its own power, like a tornado picking up momentum as it moved. Would this chaos be as destructive? How could he change the direction of things? Who could he turn to for answers? The little gale was picking up and the sky had darkened with his thoughts. Granddad and Brian had been his closest advisors. He tried to envision what they would say now. He could imagine the look of disappointment in their eyes. Brian would be telling him of the importance of school. He would also likely disapprove of Rod. Brian had never been a great fan of the Powers boys and he would never have approved of the drug scene. Brain had been the clean cut boy mother's loved to see come home with their daughters, and coaches loved to see show up for tryouts. Brain would have told him to relax, but not the way Rod did. Rod lived life like a leaf in the wind; no direction, no aim. Brian lived life like a tern on a breeze; he appeared to be floating haphazardly, but he knew exactly where he was headed. He made life look easy, something he'd inherited from Granddad. Cadiz had never nailed down that trait. He was a worrier like his dear old dad. Granddad's solution would have been to put him to work. "A boy who was busy was a boy with his mind and his hands where the devil couldn't tempt them."

As Cadiz tried to sort through the storm within, a more bodeful one was brewing outside. He did not realize until it was too late. The sea became choppy, bouncing the little craft like a cork. Without a skirt, *The Lady Seaknife* took on water, making her unstable. Cadiz tried to steer her into the waves to keep them from lapping over her sides. He could feel the water slosh about his legs. Brian had not completely finished the boat. The bulkheads had not been sealed inside and the Seaknife was taking on water at every seam. A rain blew in with the gale and pelted Cadiz's face like fine gravel. His fingers were getting numb, a feeling he did not want to remember. He crested a great wave and his heart seemed to stop as he descended nose first into the sea. In an instant he saw the furtive breaker waiting to claim him. The boat smashed hard against the rock. There was a cacophony of splintering wood, howling wind, and water. The icy Atlantic gripped him by the chest like an old nemesis. It was a nightmarish deja vu, but this time he refused to let his panic take over. He tread water, breathing deep breaths between waves and glimpsing quickly at his surroundings. A rocky ledge a few meters away offered great danger or sweet salvation, depending upon his either crashing against it or controlling his arrival. The winds were pushing him toward it. He began to swim, trying to calculate its distance and height. It was soon within reach. His lungs were aching with water and irregular breaths. The salt water bit into his eyes. He could feel his muscles rejecting his demands. A great wave smashed him into the ledge. As it did he tried to grasp hold. His numb finger tips awaked in shock as a few of his fingernails tore free, shredded on the craggy shore. He ignored the pain, forced his muscles to obey and crawled to the top of the ledge. He rolled on to the craggy bank and coughed violently, emptying his burning lungs. He crawled to a tangled and meager copse lined with moss. There Cadiz collapsed. The wind and rain taunted his little haven, but it held its ground, protecting this fallen alien visitor.

6   SURVIVAL

*C*adiz felt something lapping at his fingertips. His eyes fluttered and it took him a moment to grasp fully where he was. He sat up slowly, his every muscle straining, like taut rubber bands ready to snap. Had something been lapping at him, or was it part of a dream? He could not be certain, but the thought of some unknown creature, out there in the dusk made him shudder. He leaned on his right hand and pulled his left closer to his face. The twilight made it difficult to see, but the three missing fingernails made his hand look alien to him. The cold helped to numb the pain, but he could feel the sting of the raw, exposed flesh. His shoulder burned too. He recalled how it had bashed madly against the jagged ledge, tearing the skin and flesh from him.

Cadiz stood slowly, the scenery swirling about him, and walked from the little circle of gnarled trees. The rain had stopped and the wind had slowed to a cold hush. The crashing surf matched the pounding ache in Cadiz's head, and its cold spray matched the chill keeping hold of his frigid body. He moved inland trying to avoid the icy staccato that came with each wave. The turbulent sea had not shaken the storm. His wet jeans felt like leaden chaps and his feet squished uncomfortably in his shoes. He removed his water-logged sweatshirt, pealing it from the broken flesh of his right shoulder. He rung it out as best he could with his fingertips barking their discomfort, and put it back on. He could not imagine ever feeling warm again. He removed his shoes and repeated the process of wringing, first with his pants, then with his socks. His father's voice echoed through his mind. "Wet cotton kills, son. It takes the heat from the body. Better to not wear it at all." This was why his dad and granddad had always insisted on wearing wool socks. He always thought them old fashioned, but now he knew he should have listened.

Cadiz could not bring himself to stay stripped down. Shivering uncontrollably, he replaced his clothes and set out to get his bearings. He checked his watch. The light worked and he was grateful. Soon it would be dark and that thought made him anxious. From what he could make out, there was little sustenance in his surroundings. The barren rock offered up lichen and moss, a few twisted branches, an occasional puddle iridescent in the ashen light. About fifty meters down shore and a few meters inland he could see a jutting form. As he approached, he made out its rocky outline. Two great boulders sat at an angle, about half a meter apart at the opening and broadening southward. Behind and above them a massive shard of rock reached out from the earth, likely thrust there an ice age ago. Cadiz got close enough to peak into the mouth. Could something be living inside? He feared it was home to some beast he would not want to spook into an attack. He called out. "Hello." His voice echoed back like a distant friend. It seemed a silly thing to shout, but it was all that came to mind. To add some levity, to calm his nerves, Cadiz spoke aloud quietly, "Here bear, bear, bear... It's Goldilocks. I've come for porridge." Again, his voice sang back to him. Holding his watch light on, he ducked into the narrow opening. He squeezed through the passage, listening for the faintest sound of an occupant. The muffled sound of the surf was all he could hear. The low ceiling allowed him less than a half meter square at the entrance, but the side walls opened progressively toward the back. He duck-walked further in and listened again. The surf was only faint, near silence. It was perhaps two meters deep and would be dry and warm so long as the wind didn't come from the north. He felt cozy as he relaxed, letting his guard down a little. Except for its inky darkness, this would make a fine shelter.

He exited the cave and decided to explore the island a little further before night fell completely. The little puddles, shining here and there in the semi darkness, suddenly looked delicious. It occurred to Cadiz that this was a precious commodity, soon to be lapped up by the nightly breezes and perhaps by whatever had been licking his hand. His mind began to race. How could he collect the fresh water?

Granddad's voice spoke in his head. "Water be the main thing lads. A man can live wit'out 'is pipe, wit'out his woman, even wit'out 'is belly bein' full, but he can go no more 'n a couple days wit'out water."

Granddad had shown them how to detect a fresh water spring and how to distill fresh water from salt water. It occurred to Cadiz that if he could collect rain water, it would save him a lot of hassle and maybe even his life. It was difficult to make out the objects that littered the ground. He had so far seen no sign of humans having been here, although it was likely. He had been out at sea less than two hours when he crashed here. He estimated that he was on one of a group of small islands a few kilometers south of the accident site. It would mean he was out of the traffic lanes, but still not abandoned by civilization altogether. As he traced the shapes along the ground he could tell night was catching up with him. A three quarter moon was making an occasional appearance through grey, spent clouds.

He bent down to one of the deeper puddles and cupped the cool water into his hands. He imagined its sweet taste and took a large draught. He spit wildly as the brine bit his tongue. The sea spray had contaminated the rain water. His heart sank with his body as he dropped to the ground. Finding water would not be so easy. The fading light meant his search would have to wait for morning. A tiny flash caught his eye. About a meter and a half away something reflected light. He crawled over and began to poke at it with his healthy index finger. Plastic! He began to dig and pull. It was a discarded garbage bag, the large black ones used for lawn clippings. His sunken heart leapt to life again. Dad had told him of its insulating qualities. He had just discovered his night's bedding! He decided to seek out his shelter and wait out the night with his new found treasure. When he found the cave, he repeated the process of slipping in slowly and calling for inhabitants. When he felt confident he was not intruding on anything, he slipped out to gather the moss that surrounded the area. After several trips he felt his little nest would serve the night. He removed his shoes, wet jeans, and jacket, leaving them just outside the entrance where the wind might dry them, but the sea spray could not reach them. He included his socks and found a few large rocks to anchor everything in place. Where would a man be, shipwrecked without his pants?! Cadiz pulled out his pocketknife and ran the edge along the bottom and one side of the bag. He lay atop his moss bed and pulled more moss over him. Then he spread the open bag across the top of the moss and nestled in for the worse sleep of his life.

He shivered there for hours, wondering if anyone would be looking for him. He would have to hope Rod had phoned to apologize. When his parents discovered that he was not with Rod they would begin a search. Would they check the loft? Of course they would, eventually, wouldn't they? And in doing so they would notice the missing kayak, wouldn't they? He would have to hope for that too. He imagined the frantic phone calls, his mother's panic. Worse, he imagined their ineffectual shrugs, heard his father comment, "Good riddance. I've had enough of the b'y."

These thoughts were not helping to calm him. He turned his thoughts outward. The surf drowned out all other sounds. Could there be animals lurking just outside? A bear ready to tear him to ribbons? A mink that would scratch at his eyes once he fell asleep? This too was not helping. He needed to think of something soothing, try to relax his body into sleep. He imagined his bed at home with its full down comforter, Granddad's loft with its rich smell of tobacco, a happy homecoming…

When sleep came, his dreams unfolded like badly spliced film. Bugs crawled from the moss to claim him. Rod laughed at him and kids at school joined in, pointing and throwing chalk with their jeers. A boy with eyes of coal and skin of cinnamon pushed him toward a fire that licked at his face. An evil mink gnawed at his hand, and he watched paralyzed as it devoured each finger. The sea clutched at him and dragged him down to a horrific world of ghastly faces with hair streaming upward like kelp. One face began to take shape. He realized it was Brian crying out to him.

7   WHITTLING DESTINY

*H*e awoke with a jolt. Thin shards of light sliced through the seams that made up the cave. When his eyes adjusted, he checked his watch; 6:03 a.m. It had been a restless night of damp cold, awaking from one haunting dream only to fall into another. Cadiz was grateful to see the sunlight. He rose slowly. His tongue felt like sandpaper scraping dryly across teeth that seemed to be wearing little fuzzy sweaters. He craved his toothbrush, and his thirst made it difficult to breath. Outside, he coughed and inhaled the fresh air. A large ice berg sailed out in the distance. From afar, it looked like a small mountain taking a slow vacation from the north. Several floes escorted it like guardian satellites.

Cadiz noted a clean horizon, then took stock. His socks, shoes, jeans and coat were still damp, but much improved. He slipped on the pants and shoes, then hung the coat and socks on a gnarled shrub to dry a little more. It was a great day for exploring. He shuddered as a chill momentarily gripped him, goose flesh rippling his body. The wind blew lightly, but the sun was bright. If it held out, he would be warm and dry by the afternoon. The breeze felt soothing on his throbbing shoulder.

Taking great care with his raw fingers, he tucked down his pockets to make them comfortable. He made a great discovery. His Lifesavers! He chuckled at the irony. The sticky, wet roll could very well help to save his life. He peeled back the limp paper and pulled one from the tacky mass. With great relief, saliva flooded his mouth. He savored every second of its rum and butteriness on his tongue. It triggered a great growl from his empty belly. Margo's fine chicken had long since served its purpose.

He climbed atop his new home and looked out to sea. Small islands of rock dotted the horizon. These would help to break the waves, but they also would separate him from any traffic. The grey of the rock melded with the grey of the sea and seemed endless. He had felt loneliness in the past months, but nothing as complete as this. He sat down and pulled up his knees, a seated fetal position. He could not have felt smaller. He had pushed so many people away and now he would risk anything just to feel the warmth of another human being.

He wondered again what was happening at home. Had Rod spoken to his folks? He hoped so desperately and yet all his instincts told him no. It was Rod's nature to just let things ride. Rod would wait until Monday at school and approach him like nothing had happened. What if Cadiz didn't show up? Would Rod care? If he died out here on this rock, would Rod grieve? Or would it be like with the loss of his dad, Cadiz as just another distant memory, given little thought. If Rod hadn't called, his parents would still be cuddled, asleep under their lemon fresh sheets and downy soft comforter. In an hour the smell of coffee would fill the house mingled with the soapy clean scent of dad's shaving cream. Mom would be busy in the kitchen planning a menu; perhaps chicken or fish thawing in the sink, awaiting the crock pot. It amazed Cadiz how clearly he could see his home. Even the mustard yellow counter top with its ancient chrome moldings looked inviting. The vinyl and chrome chairs he had always resented as old and outdated were a welcome thought. Why had he always felt angry that he lived in his granddad's hand-me-down house? It seemed silly now, but he had always wanted a new house. So many of his school chums had homes with kitchen's from Better Homes and Gardens, living rooms the envy of Ikea. But what did it matter? He offered up a silent prayer that he would one day see the fifties kitchen he called home. How odd to think of such things when his mind should be on food and water.

Something was digging into his thigh. He stretched out his leg, leaned back, and reached deep into his pocket. It was his pocketknife. He pulled it out and rolled it over in his fingers. The silver ends glinted in the sunlight. The inlaid, fine, wood-grain finish shone brightly. Granddad had done a meticulous job of the hilt. Cadiz imagined the wood before it was varnished, soft as velvet. He pulled out the blade. He had owned the little knife for almost half his life and used it almost daily. He seldom really *looked* at it. The inscription on the blade, though nicked and not as shiny, was still very legible; "Let your own hand whittle your destiny." He and Granddad had never discussed the engraving, but over the years Cadiz had come to understand its meaning. He thought about it now. His destiny had truly come to be in his hands. Yet, as he thought of the preceding months, it occurred to him that he had been letting Granddad down. He had been letting his life get away from him. He had been losing control. Now, alone at sea, he would have to rely on himself. He stood and inspected his surroundings. "Time to get *whittling*," he said aloud, and climbed down to begin an expedition.

Walking the shore, he discovered he was inhabiting a small island, approximately one-hundred fifty metres by fifty metres. The south end was a great rock cliff, dropping several meters to the sea. From here it made a gradual descent northward. The east side held the rocky ledge where he had made his arrival. The opposite shore was gradual, creating a softly sloping beach in sight of a larger neighboring island to the west. This beach would be even more inviting at low tide. Just north of the center of the island stood the jagged boulder, the south wall and roof of his new home, thrusting skyward like a sail. Having mapped out the basics, Cadiz decided to crisscross the entire island to find anything that may help him survive. His main focus would be to find water, but his family had taught him that a keen eye and an open mind allowed a pig's ear to become a silken purse. He would scour the ground and will it into giving him what he needed. Cadiz began at the high south end and made a shallow zigzag northward. Scraggly wild raspberry plants teased him. They would not produce for months. His first treasure was several pieces of broken lobster trap, discarded as he had been on the east shore, but further south. The brittle fir planks would make good tinder if he ever managed to produce fire. He stowed a few of them in his cave then resumed his search where he had left off. Inland, he found a one litre plastic bottle peeking coyly out of the ground, its blue label a give away in the stark landscape. He notched the neck in his belt loop and continued.

It was tedious work walking slowly from east to west, west to east, head down, eyes fixed. Occasionally he stretched skyward. A few gulls circled, crying out to break the monotony of the surf and wind. They reminded him of homely angels, banished to guard this lonely little isle. His sweatshirt, though still damp at the seams and pocket, was finally feeling dry and he could enjoy the warmth of the sun. A few wispy clouds vied for his attention, casting the occasional light shadow, but the sun was definitely king for today. He discovered a few companions on the island. An ant colony busied itself with a dead moth, their steady rows of workers reminding him of his own task; back and forth, forth and back. A few spiders had left their targets, misted by sea spray and ready for prey. Cadiz wished he was self sufficient so as to trap his breakfast so easily. He plucked at a strand and watched the beauty of the web collapse. He plucked a second strand and watched it turn into one wispy bit of nothing. A third touch would set it off in the breeze. It took so little to create chaos from order.

He wandered to the western shore where he reached the beach, perhaps the most hospitable part of the island. Cadiz sat and enjoyed the warmth of the sand. Slick boulders at the waters edge promised to offer up mussels or periwinkles, but such a hopeful search would have to wait.

"Water be the main thing lad," again his Granddad's voice. The excitement of the Lifesaver had been momentary. Thirst had gripped his throat moments afterward and clung there still. He pulled out the empty pop bottle and went to the water's edge to rinse it off, hoping he would find a use for it soon. He noted a ripple of concentric circles just a few metres out. It was a mink. Cadiz thought of the nibbling at his hands he had felt when first awaking on the island. Could this be the culprit? He made a mental note. Should the sea offer up her bounty, the mink would not hesitate to thieve a free meal. Cadiz would have to be strategic in stowing any food. He replaced the bottle in his belt loop and went back to his task.

It had taken him most of the early morning and he was only half way through. He had found the odd trinket; an old work glove, a chipped CD, bits of trash, all likely blown in across the ice. Cadiz had seen no sign of a camp fire or other inhabitation. With the breakers that skirted the island, it was not a likely lunch counter for fisherman or families looking to picnic.

As he began a slow decent toward the north shore Cadiz, noticed red moss bright as fire in the sunlight. His heart began to race. His granddad had shown him and Brian many times that this was a good indication of fresh water. He ran toward the spot, his eyes widening as last year's rusty Labrador tea leaves encouraged his suspicions. The tender new buds meant the plant was getting nourishment! He dropped to his knees and began to claw. His raw fingertips caught the earth and he was forced to dig more gently. The layer of moss gave up easily. After digging up three or four centimeters of humus, he revealed a faint trickle slowly draining into a crevice from its sponge walls.

Cadiz could not believe his eyes. He would not be fooled with a salty mouthful again. He dipped his fingertip in the cool water and brought it to his tongue. The water was sweet and cool and wonderful. His taste buds sprang into action, his body eager to follow. This was precious stuff and had to be collected; each drop a jewel. How would he get it into the bottle? His heart sank as he peered about the landscape, waiting for an answer. The answer came, not from his surroundings, but from his pocket. He pulled out his pocketknife, and with it the pocket itself and a shiny quarter, Margo's change. He transferred the quarter to his other pocket and, using the knife he tore the pocket free – his sponge! He used his pocketknife to cut the neck of the bottle, then inverted it as a funnel. Then he set his new sponge to work.

It was a tedious process, sopping up few teaspoons of water at a time and squeezing it into the bottle. After about half a cup, he could not contain himself. He took a large swallow. It felt delicious on his lips and even better as it trickled down to his belly. It flushed the salt water and sugar from his teeth, tongue and throat. It had the taste of survival, and the effect of a giddying drug. He could do this! He could last! He did a jig and threw in the odd disco move, his hips gyrating, his arms thrust skyward. Head up he twirled around and cried back to the gulls, "I can do this!"

When the excited puppy in him was once again penned, Cadiz took clumps of the red sphagnum moss and padded his shoulder. Granddad had told him of its anti-bacterial qualities and its cool roots soothed his torn flesh. With that done, he made his way to the camp. The pocket-sponge was too slow. He would use his sock. The thought of what microscopic critters might be living in it made him cringe, but his thirst won out. He returned with the sock and would spend the rest of the morning squeezing water into the bottle.

Throughout the long, mindless task, he explored the many avenues of his thoughts. They inevitably wandered home. By now his parents would be busy with the activities brought by the day. His mind alternated between two scenarios: would they be at the hub of a flutter of rescuers, collecting information, formulating a plan, helicopter engines buzzing like mad bees? Or would it be a serene day, oblivious of their son's flight and plight? He whispered prayers for the former, but felt some comfort in the latter. He remembered spring Saturdays in the backyard. They had brought a sense that all was right with the world. A new season had come and with it all the hope of new beginnings. Brian and his friends had played rugby and invited him in. The rough and tumble game had, at first, intimidated him. But they had been careful and complimentary, at least until he had the hang of it. Then he was one of the boys. He had always admired the way his brother managed to fit him in. Brian had made it seem natural to his friends that Cadiz should belong. It had made things easier at school. His shy nature was set free by being identified as Brian's kid brother- instant allies. He had ruined all that this year with his stupid behavior. Slowly people had quit talking to him, unable to speak through the walls he had built up around him. At first the walls and his silence had been to shelter the fear, but with each person that dropped away, his fear had turned to anger; the walls as much to hold him in as to keep them out. He knew they blamed him, and their distance only confirmed it. He hated their judging eyes and furtive glances. More than that, he hated that they were right.

So now, here he sat, sopping water in a dirty sock. Once more the sea had tried to claim him. Once more he had slipped through its icy clutches. But to what end? Was his survival just a prolonged punishment? Was the sea only waiting to take him after he had suffered. Would she wait until he was thin and weak and broken to exact her toll? Self-pity seized Cadiz and he began to weep. The contradictions of his life swirled inside him, climbing like a funnel from his stomach into his brain. He had longed to die, as he should have that day in October, and yet last night, he had fought and won his ground. He had wanted to run away from the staring faces at school, and yet he had resented his dad dragging them to Yellowknife. He had envied Rod and his apparent flippancy, and yet in the end he had found it senseless, almost repulsive. The giddiness of finding water had been fleeting. He had shelter, he had water, but so what? He was alone on a rock; a prison, with walls of water, had replaced the one he had built around himself. He had finally gotten what he deserved, what he had almost longed for. What was he to do now? The sobs came harder, surging up from his belly. Cadiz called out to the sea, "What?! What do I do? What do you want from me?!"

He smeared away the tears, but they kept coming. His anger pulled him, like a tangible force, to his feet. He clenched his fists and shook them at his little island world. He kicked the moss and little shrubs. He felt acutely aware that he looked like a small child in a tantrum, but what did it matter? No one could see him. He was alone. So alone. So bitterly alone that it made him feel sick to his stomach. The rage past and he slumped to the ground. He sobbed quietly.

"I miss you Brian," he whispered. "You too Granddad. I'm so sorry. So sorry."

He pulled the knife from his pocket, pulled open the blade and read the inscription.

Let your own hand whittle your destiny.

"Granddad, how?" he asked of the blade. "I whittled so many mistakes, how do I fix them? How?"

No answer came; only the wind, the surf, the gulls.

8 LIFE & DEATH

*C*adiz realized he'd been a fool to have paddled out of the harbor "maverick," without the safety of a spray skirt or life-vest. He also realized that he'd be a greater fool if he did not get a grip on his emotions. Laying about crying and beating up on the plant life was not going to do him any good. With his pop bottle finally full, he returned to the cave and set his sock out to dry. With bottle in hand, he made his way to the beach, in hope of finding food. Nine Lifesaver candies were not going to sustain him and low tide should offer up something of interest. His shoulder was throbbing in time to his heartbeat, but both were nearly drowned out by the rumblings in his stomach. His crying jag had lost him valuable water. While tears cleansed the soul, his body could not afford too many such launderings.

The beach was hosting a few gulls and Asprey who quickly vacated upon Cadiz's arrival. He set down his water and cautiously approached the slick boulders that skirted the beach. Thick Knotted-wrack kelp covered the rocky shore-line, floating like cheap plastic grapes in the tide. They would be the best bet for finding mussel and periwinkle. Nature had tried hard to mask the blue mussels against the blue-black rock, but Cadiz's keen eyes sought them out. He brought the bottom of his sweatshirt over his left forearm and created a basket. Checking his footing, Cadiz then reached carefully for the mussels. The rocks were slippery and jagged; a broken ankle could be a death sentence out here. Being cautious of the spiny sea urchins that shared the habitat, he tore the mussels stuck like Velcro from the rock, and pinched off a few periwinkles too. His dad had shown he and Brian how to crack open 'wrinkles to bait cunner, ocean perch, on the wharf. He was going to have to resort to eating fish bait. To think that he had turned his nose up at fish and brews, Jig's dinner, cooked beets, olives…and now his mouth was watering at the thought of the raw, slimy little morsels hiding in their shells.

He sat carefully, so as not to dump his harvest. They might be gritty enough; no need to add more sand to his diet. He pulled a mussel from his makeshift basket and inserted his blade into the shell. With a hard twist of the blade the shell popped open to reveal a gruesome dish. The mussels Cadiz had eaten at home were always steamed and he was expecting a firm morsel. His throat tightened as he looked down at the open shell, filled with a colourful and gelatinous mass. The repulsive smell of raw fish flared his nostrils and he stared long at the slick, rusty-orange mass. A cocoa dusted saddler watched curiously from the shore. Lured by a cheap lunch, the pigeon-toed gull wandered closer.

Cadiz tossed him an opened mussel, "Go ahead buddy."

The gull looked like he was performing a piece of the tango as it made a few timid steps forward, then one back. Eventually it reached its prize. Cadiz laughed as it fought the shell, swinging the mussel from side to side.

"You're a bright one," he said with sarcasm, "think I'll call you Rod."

Cadiz cracked a second shell and again grimaced at its contents. He looked at his new feathered companion, "Well, you seem right enough, Rod. Guess I best give it a try, eh?"

With resolve and his breath on hold, he popped it into his mouth. The raw egg texture made his tongue retreat to the bottom of his mouth. He swallowed hard and took a large tug from the water bottle. The little blob seemed to be doing gymnastics in his belly. He sat motionless, certain it was going to wriggle back up his esophagus. When the nausea ebbed, he decided to try a 'wrinkle. Bashing its tough exterior with a rock, Cadiz picked through the shells and popped a rubbery morsel into his mouth. He tried to imagine the bite was his mom's to-die-for brownie bites, but the smell and texture told him otherwise. He had heard of escargot and tried to convince himself he was not eating fish bait or gull food. Images of erasers soaked in sardine oil came to mind. He tossed a second mussel to the gull. As it approached, he noticed it was missing its left eye. "The black-backs been at ya little fella? He asked. The bird ignored him and fought the mussel from its shell.

And so the two of them dined; Rod wrestling so as to quickly gulp each bite, Cadiz gagging and flushing each slimy blob down with a swig of water. When the feast was over, the gull took flight, salt and cocoa against the light blue sky. Cadiz relished a Lifesaver, letting it melt on his tongue to outdo the fishy taste still hiding in the grooves of his taste buds. He found a twig laying nearby and used his knife to fray the end. His father had shown him this trick once, when in a rush to pack, the toothbrushes had been forgotten. It had been a four day camping trip and his mother, although all for roughing it, was not about to become so uncivilized as to bypass brushing her teeth. Cadiz and his dad had made twig toothbrushes for the whole family.

His teeth brushed and his belly relatively satisfied, Cadiz lay back in the warm sand. Down close to the ground, the breeze disappeared and he felt wonderfully warm. He closed his eyes and watched sun spots dance beneath his eyelids. He felt proud of himself. He had reigned in his emotions. He had found food and water. After a little sun bath, he would tackle fire.

Cadiz awoke from a deep dreamless sleep. The kind of awakening where it feels like one's bones have evaporated and the flesh is as heavy as lead. He felt something warm between his chest and arm, but the sleepy paralysis only allowed him to focus his eyes, leaving him motionless. Much to his surprise he found his gull-friend nesting comfortably beside him.

Cadiz found his voice, "Well, if it ain't me buddy Rod."

The gull popped up like it had tightly coiled springs for legs. Warily it hopped out of reach, but continued to stare with its one good eye. Cadiz rose slowly, nudging his body to do his bidding. His shoulder still ached from its impact against the rocks. His lower back complained too, from the many hours of sitting, sponging at the water hole. He stretched out skyward and noticed the sun had made slow progress toward the western horizon. Checking his watch, he guessed he had about four hours to dark. He smiled at his new companion.

"You're a friendly one. Not quite white yet, are ya, pup?" Cadiz could see this gull was a juvenile, not just hatched, but not yet ready to be on its own.

"What says we tackle fire? You got any matches hidden in those feathers? How 'bout a lighter?"

The gull tilted its head, good eye toward Cadiz, as if to question the sanity of asking a bird such a question, then retreated to the sky.

"Ya, didn't think so," replied Cadiz. "Guess I'll have to do it the hard way."

He began a search for just the right branch. With only a few gnarled shrubs around, it would be difficult to find one straight and long enough for a bow. He began his zigzag approach, this time beginning from the northern most point. He rummaged through the little copse he had lodged in on his arrival. Eventually he found a piece of driftwood about a metre long and a centimetre in diameter. He began his trek back to the beach when something near the northwestern shore caught his eye.

A dark heap lay on the rocks, perhaps a washed up net or buoy. Its edges seemed too round to be a boulder and he did not recall seeing it when he had made the many treks to the spring. As he neared, he realized it was a seal. Hooded seals were known to be docile when approached, but Cadiz was surprised to find it staring up at him as he hovered. Its eyes lacked the bright shine he had seen on the seals sunning near the harbor in the village and it occurred to him that the animal was sick or hurt. He circled it and noted a large gash like its throat had been slashed. It had been victim to either man or nature. It could have been many things, but Cadiz was not skilled enough to decipher the wound, only to note that it was nasty. He had heard of seals getting caught in ghost nets, but an aggressive mink could also do this kind of damage. A grazing from the bullet of a poacher was a possibility too.

The animal looked at him with its sorrowful and somewhat clouded eyes. Cadiz moved a ways away and sat staring. This could be his *silken purse*. A seal meant no more slimy mollusks sliding down his throat. It meant a warm pelt under his garbage bag. It meant oil, for fuel, should he ever conquer fire. It meant death on his hands. Perhaps the suffering beast would welcome death? He had a fleeting vision of himself smashing a rock over the head of the helpless creature and the thought made him tighten. Perhaps the animal would die without his help? He sat staring, the images of warmth, food, fuel and death replaying again and again in his head. Judging from the tide line, he decided the seal wasn't going anywhere for a while. He would tackle fire and return later to check on the animal. He could postpone his decision and hope it would be made for him.

He resumed his journey to the beach, driftwood in hand, stopping at the cave for a few planks from the broken lobster trap he had collected earlier. He rummaged above the beach line and collected paper-dry eel grass kelp. Scooping some of the sand, he dug a small, shallow pit and placed one of the planks from the lobster trap inside. Using his knife he notched his driftwood about two centimetres from either end. Being gentle with his nail-less fingers, he carefully removed one of his shoe laces and tied it to each notched end to create his bow. He set the grass on top of the plank. Now all he needed was a stick about forty centimeters long.

Rod had landed a few meters away and was eyeing Cadiz's progress suspiciously. Cadiz once again set out searching, but this time avoiding the seal that haunted the shallow recesses of his thoughts. It did not take long to find a fairly straight stick of the right length and width. He wrapped the shoelace once around the stick, then squatted to begin his work. He held the stick perpendicular to the old plank and buried it in the dry grass. He held the bow parallel to the ground and began to move it back and forth, like the old buck saw he and his dad had used while camping. His dad and granddad had explained this process to Cadiz and Brian, but he'd never actually tried it.

He and Brian had big plans to experiment with it one summer afternoon, but they had been sidetracked when they were able to start fire with a magnifying glass. Things had gotten out of hand when the back lawn had caught fire. He was about ten then. He could still remember his mom coming around from the front yard, her eyes had grown to the size of tea saucers, and she had bolted for the garden hose. By the time his dad had arrived home from work, an ugly black scar through the back yard was the only evidence of their misdeed. In retrospect the excitement had been worth the week-long grounding; however, it still made him queasy to think of what could have happened, had it been a drier summer. Had it reached the house, a grounding would have been the least of their problems. After that day, neither he nor Brian had had any real ambition to set another fire outside of a camping pit.

He kept the bow moving. The trick was to be quick and constant so as to create friction. This friction would in turn cause heat and igniting the grass and leaves. With a little oxygen from his breath this would burst into flame and he could add more of the dry fir planks from the old lobster traps. This all seemed so easy in his mind's eye. In truth his inner shoulder was beating a steady tattoo and his hands were already getting sore. The grass looked no more ready to burst into flames than he did.

When he could push his weary arm no longer, he took a break and walked to the cave. He had a small sip of water and rummaged through the stash of treasures he'd collected earlier. He found the old glove and tried it on for size. The fit was a bit large, but that gave his raw fingers a bit of breathing space. It was dirty inside and out. He could not wash it and wear it wet, as it would soften the skin on his hands. His young hands were too soft as it was and he wished he had the tough, callused working man's hands of his dad. He would have to wear the dirt-filled glove and remember to soak his hand in the ocean later. The salt water would act as an antibiotic, should his nail-less fingers find bacteria inside the filthy glove. Slightly refreshed, he returned to try again at fire.

As he worked, Rod poked about the beach and took short flights around the island, always returning to watch Cadiz's labourings. The rhythm of the bow brought back memories for Cadiz. As his arm pumped methodically back and forth he recalled autumn with the buck-saw. Brian and Granddad had been one team, Cadiz and his father another. The four of them had trucked into the interior to find dead fall for the fireplace. Last September had been particularly mild and they had set out for a full day. The forest had been cool and peaceful. The sun had cast dappled shadows over them and the steady hum of the saws had sounded like a melody.

About midday, Dad had been called by nature to "do

his business." He had disappeared into the bush with toilet paper and magazine in hand. Cadiz and Granddad had taken it as an opportunity for a much needed water break and rest. A twinkle had glinted in Brian's eye, which meant he was hatching a plan. Smiling, he motioned Cadiz toward the truck and whispered his idea. Quietly they pulled a large black tarp off the back of the truck and nestled beneath, Brian in the lead, Cadiz following closely behind. They maneuvered their way silently through the trees, making a large arch to come upon their father from the rear. They could see him slouched and settled and reading. Cadiz fought hard to stifle his giggles. When they were a few metres away, Brian began to grunt loudly and picked up the pace. John looked back, his eyes widening. He sprang into the air, the magazine fluttering up, then down like a broken bird. He shouted "Bear!" and at the same time began to run, his pants skirted around his ankles and his belt buckle flopping madly behind him, like the head of an epileptic snake. The boys lumbered through the forest, Brian grunting, Cadiz giggling wildly. When they reached camp, Granddad was doubled over with laughter, tears streaming down his cheeks. John grinned shamefully and pulled up his pants. It was a story he knew would plague him for years.

Cadiz felt the smile on his face and it felt good. The memory had pushed him to continue, but his hands began to scream their displeasure. He stopped to look. Ugly blisters had broken on his glove-less hand, leaving hot red gashes. He pulled the glove from his other hand and noted that the palm was red and sore and had begun to blister. His heart sank. He would have to give up on fire for tonight.

Deserting his fire-starting endeavor he went to the water's edge to soak his throbbing hands. The icy water soothed his wounds, but not his spirits. He had looked so forward to success; to its warmth and comfort, to hot food, to the confidence of survival it would award him. Rod-the-gull flapped down nearby and cocked his head to watch Cadiz at the shore.

"Hey. Ol' boy. Where're ya to?" Cadiz asked him.

The bird pointed his beak northward as if in answer. The struggling seal came to the forefront of Cadiz's thoughts. He hoped that the gull or other birds were not pestering the dying seal. He considered the mink he had seen earlier and wondered if it would be awaiting an easy meal.

Hastily, he made his way back to the seal. It opened its eyes when he came between it and the late afternoon sun. The eyes were solemn, heavy and milky.

"'Eh ol' boy how are ya?" Cadiz asked in a gentle voice. "You got it pretty bad didn't ya fella?"

Cadiz crouched close to the animal this time. There was no indication that it had been badgered by scavengers. Only its eyes and the ugly tear in its neck gave evidence of its suffering. Cadiz's belly growled and he felt guilty; his body's needs betraying his tender heart. He paced across the dried kelp and rock, trying to make a decision. What would Brian say? Granddad? His father? His mom? He realized that, unanimously, they would have agreed that the seal should die.

For centuries these animals had sacrificed themselves to the survival of the inhabitants of this land, but Cadiz wondered if he had it in him to take the life of another creature, especially one with such human eyes. He had killed many a fish, crab and lobster, but they never really looked you in the eyes. Granddad and Brain had hunted moose, but he'd never had the heart for it. He enjoyed the long-legged, clumsy looking beasts with their caricature profiles. His thoughts suddenly turned to the tender moose roasts his mom prepared and saliva flooded his mouth at the thought of juicy meat slathered in mushroom gravy. A swirl of hunger and guilt swam in his belly, but guilt had no purpose here. The seal was survival. He had no other choice.

He dropped to his knees and lifted a large rock in both hands. He practiced bringing it down on a tuft of moss. If he was going to do this, he would have to make it as quick and as painless as possible. He could pacify himself with thoughts of putting the animal out of its misery. If he failed, and bludgeoned the poor thing, he would have endless new nightmares to add to his collection.

After several blows to the mossy clump, his adrenaline was in full rush. He rose and turned to the seal. This time it did not raise its head nor eyes to him. Hope bubbled to the surface- his adrenaline faltered. Could it be dead? He leaned down and placed a hand on its side. The seal's eyes flickered open and it turned slightly in Cadiz's direction. Cadiz pulled the rock high overhead then brought it down, it crashed against the rocks. He had lost his nerve at the last moment and pulled left to miss the pathetic creature. He breathed hard and tears rivered down his cheeks. He rose, and paced back and forth a few feet from the scene. He had to do this. He had to!

Anger raged inside; anger at his own weakness. He needed to leash the angry dog that often raced within him, use its savage edge to drive him. He envisioned those laughing frat boys at the back of the bus. He pictured Rod leaping from the top step. He saw Mr. Clark spewing degradation and spittle. Cadiz let loose the angry dog. He reached for the boulder and dropped to his knees. The rock swung high overhead, between his hands. He took aim and with all his might brought the rock down. The primitive weapon struck its mark hard and fiercely. Crimson sprang from the seal's dark skull and the animal went limp.

Cadiz felt its flank again, nothing. He put his head to its side. Quiet. Cadiz deflated. Tears mercifully blurred his vision. Like so many before him, Cadiz offered up sorrow and thanksgiving. This creature with its sweet eyes and sweet flesh had once again given itself over to the sustenance of man. Cadiz breathed deeply and ran his sleeve across his salty face. When his heart slowed and his eyes cleared, he busied himself with the task at hand.

He pulled the dead seal to higher land and rolled it onto its back. With his pocketknife he made a long incision from tail through sternum. Next he cut around the flippers, then the head, using the wound as a cut mark. He had seen this kind of work done before. His mother had skinned rabbits and his granddad had been part of the seal hunts of long ago. It was Granddad that had taught he and Brian the importance of finding both sadness and gratitude in all hunting and fishing ventures. His father had reminded the boys of this too. Cadiz felt tears welling up and decided it was best concentrate on the food and pelt.

He scrapped the knife carefully between the flesh and hide of the animal. The knife slipped, nicking the pretty pelt. He took care, but his inexperienced hand made a few more holes before he was finished. Finally, he peeled the hide from sinew and muscle, making for a ghastly sight – the head still clothed in fur, the body naked. He turned his back on the carcass and used the discarded CD as an ulu to scrape the last bits of membrane and flesh from the hide.

When finished the flipper holes provide perfect armholes. Cadiz turned it fur side in and slipped it on. He could not help but feel that his family would be proud of him, despite the few nicks he had made. He was a regular Paleo-Eskimo! It occurred to him that when he was rescued the pelt would make a fine Mother's Day gift. His mother was an adept seamstress and could create something of real beauty from the hide.

Now he turned to the mass of fatty flesh behind him. The small pocket knife would mean he would have to cut the animal into several small pieces. He would also have to find a way to protect this important resource from predators. If he was not careful, all his hard work and turmoil would result in mink and bird food.

The sun was slowly being swallowed by the landscape when he finally had the seal carved and stashed in a crevice several meters from his cave. He piled a few boulders atop to protect his cache, then pushed the carcass out to sea and watched the birds circle and swoop at the feast it provided. He would have to dry meat tomorrow to keep it from spoiling. With a little luck, he may even be able to smoke it over a fire.

He had almost finished his water with the thirst the job had created. He took time to rest at the spring, enjoying the slow work of refilling the bottle. Night was upon him and he would need to collect more moss for his bed. A three quarter moon illuminated the isle and he was able to pad his nest quiet nicely. With that done, he took a chunk of seal meat and perched himself atop his cave.

He pared away a fatty layer and sliced himself a thin piece of the seal. It smelled fishy, but the texture was much improved over the slick jiggly mussels. He popped the piece into his mouth and chewed. It was definitely raw flesh and definitely from the sea, but not all that bad. Cadiz reasoned that if it had served the Inuit all those centuries, it had to be food. It would take some getting used to, but with a swallow of water Cadiz felt like he was finally having a meal. Rod perched nearby and Cadiz shared his bounty.

"Not half bad, eh buddy?" Cadiz asked. "Don't forget to be thanking the seal now. If not for him you mighta been my next choice. I may not be much with a snare, but you're not the quickest thing I seen on this island."

The gull gulped great slabs of meat, then settled into a mossy knot. Again, Cadiz finished his entree with a Lifesavor. Seven of his eleven candies remained. With luck, his parents were already searching. If not, they would certainly start seeking him out tomorrow evening when he would not return for supper and the preparations for Monday's meeting.

Again, a dark cloud invaded his thoughts. They would seek him out wouldn't they? If they thought he ran away, would they go after him or sigh with relief? He pushed the image away and smiled. He would be rescued and a school meeting would be the least of their concerns. He pictured Ms. Simmons, copper hair ablaze, giving him a warm greeting and gushing her happiness at his safe return. The smile faded. Would he have a safe return? He had shelter and food. Worst case scenario, he would have to last until the waters warmed and try to swim from island to island. Could he last until freeze up and simply walk home? He looked around and noted the vast loneliness that engulfed him. Five months here? Best push those thoughts far away. Rescue would come, and soon.

He pulled a stone from his pocket. He had found it

while stashing the seal meat and thought it suitable for honing his pocketknife. The knife had served him well, but it was becoming dull with its many tasks. As he honed he looked out to sea. It swirled and rolled, steely in the moon light. He wondered what they were up to in the port of Cadiz. Would he get there one day? It would be nice to sit on its shore and look out to sea imagining this little isle looking back. He would do his best to whittle his destiny to include such a trip. He would do his best to whittle his way back home. He swiveled southeast. If he could walk on water, he could easily walk home. He knew the way, but the water was far too cold to swim his way from island to island until he reached the harbor. As he could neither walk, fly, nor swim, he would have to wait.

He tested the sharpened blade on his inner upper arm, as Granddad had shown him years before. All the old timers in the village wore little bald spots there, where for years they had tested their blades. Cadiz was not yet hairy enough to show the wear. He had envied Brian when his arm had begun to show the mark – a right of passage that was not so far off.

He slid down the rock and watched Rod disappear into a sky of stars and iron clouds. A floe glided by like a great shadow. He climbed into the cave and once again nestled in for the night. It took only minutes before the moss felt warm. The sounds outside were muffled, but ominous. It reminded him of long nights as a little boy, watching shadows and listening to the wind howl across the roof. Then he would tiptoe over to Brian's bed and slide in beside him. He pulled his knees up close and imagined his brother beside him in the darkness. Sleep came quickly, like a much needed friend.

Cadiz sat in a boat, the water around him a sheet of glass and the sun warm on his face. He looked out over the starboard side and saw a figure bobbing out on the surface of the water. A smaller figure surfaced beside it, then submerged. The two began to move closer, one just beneath the surface, the other clearly a man.

Brian! It was Brian! He stopped a few metres away and frolicked in the water with a seal. Cadiz shouted to him and Brian waved wearing a bold grin. Cadiz began laughing as he watched the seal pull Brian along, the two performing a circus act. Brian hammed it up, slapping the water and spitting a fountain into the air. They came right next to the boat and Cadiz reached out to grab his brother by the hand. When he looked down, Brian and the seal were disappearing beneath the surface. He reached down. Brian smiled, staring wide eyed beneath the water. He reached back, but only to wave. The seal took him deeper and deeper until they were gone. Cadiz sat staring into the water. The ripples died and once again he was alone in the stillness.

He woke, shaken by the image. The darkness engulfed him in sharp contrast to the bright sunlight of his dream. He felt strangely pacified by the thought of Brian escorted to his watery grave by a companion as sweet as a seal. He realized now that the seal of his dream had worn a scar, a jagged line across his neck. Cadiz rolled over and hoped the night would once again offer up peaceful images of his brother.

9   BEOTHUK TREASURE

*C*adiz rose with the sun. It looked to be another day of fine weather, perfect for drying his seal meat. He squatted low, arranging the moss and garbage bag, when he teetered on his haunches and fell backward. His hand dropped onto what he at first thought were stones rolled to the edge of the inner west wall. He noted their smoothness, however, and pulled one up in his hand when he rose back onto his feet. He held it in the morning light pouring through the crevice on the east side. It was no bigger in diameter than a loonie coin and perhaps half a centimetre thick. Cadiz could make out a distinct shape; that of wings. He ran his hand along the wall and discovered three more of the tiny figurines. He went outside and climbed atop the cave to get the full effect of the bright sunlight. The figures were carved and rock hard. Cadiz could not be certain if they were of rock or fossilized wood or bone. The second figure seemed to be the rear view of an upright bear, the third a seal nose pointed skyward and the forth antlers.

All four showed great detail for their size, rubbed with ochre, now a rusty red. Tiny slashes had been made to depict the wings of a bird. The seal had notches sliced for the flippers. Cadiz remembered his school studies in which they had learned of the many first nations of Canada. He had been particularly interested in the Beothuk, as they were native to Newfoundland, and sadly, no longer in existence. He had researched them and knew that it was their tradition to use ochre and to bury their dead in natural rock formations. He had also discovered that they buried their dead with carvings to take into the next world. Could he have discovered an ancient burial site? His heart began to thump more heavily. He eyed the little carvings wondering if they could really be that ancient. But if so, where were the bones? He supposed that it was possible that they had been removed by animals at some point. Mink were certainly not known to stand on ceremony. He pocketed his new treasure and checked the cave for further findings. He let his fingertips do the searching, sweeping along the caves interior perimeter. On the crook of the southwestern edge his hand brushed along two more stones, these ones rougher. Likely just pebbles, Cadiz nonetheless carried them outside to inspect them more closely. His eyes widened when he realized the full extent of his discovery.

He heard his father's voice, "Radiated iron pyrite me son, fire-stones to the Beothuk." His father had shown him such stones, explaining that the Beothuk had smacked them together to create sparks for fire. Cadiz had just found another chance at fire! Last night's seal feast was far better than slime ridden mussels, but how grand this would be! His mouth watered at the thought of hot Labrador tea, steamed mussels, and roasted seal. He envisioned a warm fire this evening and best of all he could envision the helicopters spotting his blaze and setting down to scoop him homeward.

He checked on his seal stash and noted Rod circling overhead. Drying the meat could wait. Better yet he could have smoked meat in no time! With his heart still racing at the thought of his find, Cadiz collected several of the lobster trap planks and sat outside the cave splintering them into small kindling. Reaching for a plank, Cadiz narrowly missed contact with a *skiver*. The coiled metal bait hook jutted out about eight centimetres, its rusty coating threatening Tetanus. Cadiz set the plank inside making a mental note; perhaps it would come in handy for fishing or something.

When he had sufficient kindling, he took one small piece and used his newly sharpened knife to create a pile of very fine shavings. The breeze tried to lap at them, but he huddled down close to his task. Pulling the flint from his pocket he began to hammer one piece onto the other, atop the pile of shavings. He hammered again and again, but with little effect. He tried swiping the rocks across one another. Still, ineffectual. He tried rubbing the rocks together. Nothing. He tried combinations: Rub, swipe, hammer, hammer, swipe, hammer, swipe, rub, rub, rub.

With a loud curse Cadiz threw the rocks to the ground. He stomped around, tossing a few more choice words out to sea. Why was it so difficult?! He had tried the bow, now the pyrite. Was he that stupid?! He had been offered up two chances and was blowing them both.

"I want cooked food!" he shouted at no one.

"I want to be warm!" he shouted even louder.

"I want to go home!" Now he was screaming.

It was Sunday. His parents would find him missing any time now. Perhaps they already had, but didn't care. He could feel the dog inside him again. It was chasing its tail, sending him in a swirl of sorrow, anger, and confusion. It needed to run, and Cadiz knew he would have to leash it or give it room. He ran to the beach, grabbed handful after handful of rock and pelted it into the high surf. The sea seemed to laugh at his threat – swallowing the little rocks with ease.

With his energy zapped, Cadiz tramped back to his stash. He pulled up a piece of seal, sliced off several thin pieces and gnawed on them as he went to the cave for water. Rod peered down from atop the cave and Cadiz tossed him a slice of seal and a mumbled greeting. His bottle was nearing three quarters empty. He would have to return to the spring. The thought of the long process of sponging dampened his spirits further. He hoped desperately that his parents had sent out a search party. At the spring he chewed on a few tea leaves. They were last year's crop, rusted and bitter, but edible. In a few months he could eat berries, but he could not imagine the loneliness of months on this island. Rod made a graceless landing and bounced around the periphery.

"You aren't much for conversation, pal," Cadiz noted.

The two little castaways spent the morning there; Cadiz sponging, Rod taking quick flights as if practicing his landings.

By noon Cadiz knew the tide would be ebbing, almost at its lowest.

"Come on, buddy." Cadiz called to the bird. "Lets see what's cookin' at the shore. Maybe the tide left us a yacht or a Big Mac."

Cadiz was shocked by what he saw. The tide had left a bridge to the neighbouring island. He hadn't noticed it the previous day as he had likely missed the tide at its lowest point. It was slightly covered with water, but shallow enough that, with a few slabs of rock and a little care, he could easily make it across.

He dashed back near his cave where he knew he could find the thin sheets of rock he would need. After a half dozen trips he had built up a little bridge and was ready to traverse it. He would have to be quick as the tide would return and leave him stranded.With great caution he stepped on to the first stone. It wobbled unsteadily. The second stone was better. The third was not as flat and offered more of a challenge. Cadiz made sure he had his footing with the right before lifting the left. As he went to lower his left the rock teetered and his heart lurched into his throat. He splayed his arms for balance and waited for his body to steady. His heart pounding greater with each step, he thought it might break from his chest when he finally arrived at the opposite shore.

He quickly trotted across to the far west side in hopes that he might see a familiar piece of the mainland. Instead he found more ocean with islands pooled among it. He walked the outer edge, eyes sweeping the landscape as it had on the first day. He looked for signs of life, useful garbage, food, anything that would at least keep him alive, at best, get him home. He found another garbage bag trapped in a *krumholtz*, a thicket of bristly Damson.

Once cleaned, the bag would come in handy to store his seal meat. Near the northwestern shore he spotted a knot of ashen eel grass. A neon orange peeked out from beneath, clearly man-made. Cadiz picked up his pace, making a slow jog toward the heap. He grabbed a piece of driftwood, ready to ply the stringy grass away from his find. He froze when he saw the bloated human hand half covered by tendrils of eel grass, tangled like heaps of wet cassette tape ribbon.

An argument ensued inside his head. *It wasn't a hand. It was his imagination. It must be something else. Steady boy. No, I know what I see! No, you're being childish, letting your imagination run wild. Be a man. Investigate. But what if it is a body? Well, its isn't. This isn't a horror movie. This is real life. People don't just find dead bodies laying around.*

Cadiz inched closer. Beneath a crisscross of tangled leaves, he could see a man's face, discoloured and eyeless. The sockets swimming with tiny sea lice. Cadiz dropped the driftwood and raced away. He felt the seal and bile lurching up his throat, abandoning his body as if trying to get further away from the horror he had just witnessed. A terror clutched at him as it occurred to him that Brian's body had never been recovered. They had creped the sea floor and discovered that the anchor had dragged his brother off the shoal and into the great abyss. The sky began to twist above him and he felt the hard stone of the ground grind into his knees. He fell to his palms and gasped for air. Could it be Brian?

Cadiz wiped his face with his sleeve and sat back trying to get focused. The nausea teased at his stomach, but the sky had stopped tilting. As he refocused, he allowed himself to envision the body. Brian had deserted his shoes and jacket to rescue him. He remembered the shoes bouncing along the bottom of the boat and he had worn the jacket home. This body was wearing some kind of snowsuit; its reflective orange trim had lured him here. Cadiz realized it must have been the snowmobiler that had gone missing in December. He remembered his parents talking about a family devastated when the father had been lost through the ice only two weeks before Christmas. Cadiz could not face a dead body. No matter how cold he grew, he would not wear a dead man's coat.

He rose slowly, testing his shaking legs. He took a few deep breaths, and headed for the bridge. He could explore the island another day. He had enough adventure for today.

Once back at the cave he took a long chug of water, rinsing his mouth, but not the memory of what he'd witnessed. A shudder went through him and he tried to shake the memory from his body. He could not help but to look back repeatedly, awaiting an orange rubber glove or a bloated hand gripping his shoulder. He fought the urge to cry. He feared that if he started he may never stop. Wasn't it bad enough that he was stuck out here alone, now he had to look death in its void eyes? He needed to get busy to turn his thoughts away from the gruesome scene.

He decided to give the pyrite stones another chance. The soggy mottled face kept pushing its way into his thoughts, but he forced them back to the job at hand. The pounding of the stones kept him company and he had to keep his focus on his hands so as not to drive the stones into his thumb or fingers. His patience wavered after half an hour and he walked to the beach to try the bow. This too offered respite from the horror, but no fire except for the burning in his raw hands. It was only mid afternoon and he felt like the day had aged him a decade.

He wondered if he should have braved the body and searched it. Perhaps he could have found something useful like a lighter or matches. He feared touching the corpse. His dad had explained to him how bodies sink in salt water, but eventually, filled with gases in the stomach and lungs, bloat to the surface. The winter ice acts as a cooler, Dad had explained, slowing decomposition. Cadiz knew that by now tiny sea creatures feeding would have made the body very fragile. He did not want to be responsible for it falling apart, nor present when it happened. A shiver climbed his spine and he was quite certain it had nothing to do with the clouds creeping up from the horizon.

Remembering the found bag he had trailing out of his back pocket, he washed it and spent time slicing the meat into jerky-thin strips. These he placed on the top of his cave, open to the sun and wind. Unfortunately it left them open to the ants and birds as well. He would have to stand watch. He was not high enough from the ever-nosy minks either. It did not take long before he spotted one nearby, up on its haunches sniffing the air.

He spent the remainder of the afternoon guarding the drying seal. He lay on his back waving the root end of a large piece of driftwood. It clawed at the sky like a live scarecrow. Occasionally he burst into song, to frighten off the wildlife and ghosts and to counter the surf that had become a constant irritation. To occupy himself he found scenes, faces, and animals in the approaching clouds. They were billowy and white offering up many possibilities; ships with full sails, clowns with ruffled collars, a rabbit with a missing ear, a turtle trapped on its back. Cadiz shared his findings with the gull and Rod sat listening from a large piece of driftwood. From what Cadiz could remember of Granddad's lessons, these clouds promised only the benign images and no rain. He tried to close his eyes to rest, but the void sockets stared back at him. He could hear the tide filling the many creases of the coastline. Supper time was arriving with the cloud and surf. His parents would be expecting him now.

10 MISSING

I t had been a busy weekend of spring cleaning. Rose had spent most of it indoors airing linens, and dusting the crooks and crannies that fill with winter's pollution of furnace dust, shed skin, and the like. John had been outside clearing the shed, readying the lawnmower, and tilling the flower beds.

Rose stood in the door frame of the boys' room. She had not yet grown accustomed to thinking of it as Cadiz's room. Brian's things had been packed or given away, but his bed and night table remained, the tidy blanket a quiet reminder of his absence. She knew Cadiz would not like her mussing through the room and decided to wait for his return. She turned her attention to preparing supper and went to the kitchen to wash vegetables.

John sat in a lawn chair in the front yard, facing the harbor. He twirled the pipe in his hands. It had been his father's, and John had planned to bury it with him. At the last minute he had taken it from the old man's pocket and tucked it in his own, keeping it with him like an act of defiance over death. Death claimed his father, but a part of Cadiz Senior would remain behind. John stuffed the pipe with tobacco, lit it, and took a puff. He enjoyed the smell and the memories it conjured, much more than the act itself. He turned his thoughts to his youngest son and hoped against hope that the boy was merely going through a phase, that his moodiness was the curse of adolescence and nothing more. Logic washed over his hope and told him that the boy had endured too much. Cadiz's suffering was beyond that of normal adolescence. They would move from the harsh memories, carrying only the good ones with them. Cadiz would meet new friends and the new surroundings would help him to heal.

A large berg out in the distance looked like a young mountain that had wandered off from its mother. John had always marveled at how the great masses of ice sailed so effortlessly by each spring. His pipe gone out, John looked at his watch. Supper time. He wandered to the house and found Rose at the kitchen counter.

"Could ya light the barbeque?" asked Rose on seeing him enter. "I thought you men might like a steak for a change."

"Hmmm, sounds good" replied John, reaching in his pocket for the matches.

"Where is that delinquent boy of ours?" he asked.

"I expect him in any minute," said Rose trying to sound confident. Inside she prayed he would be on time. If he wasn't, there would be arguing. As much as Cadiz would be in trouble, she knew John would hold her responsible for letting the boy stay away all weekend when he was in such hot water already. She bundled up the tinfoil packages, grabbed the steaks that had been marinating in the fridge, and set off to the barbeque. John had it lit and was fiddling with his pipe. She was pleased that he seemed to spend more time rolling it in his fingers than he ever did smoking it.

"Well, its been a productive day," said Rose. "I got rid of a bit of clutter," she added, hoping to help his mood.

"Aye, me too," he replied. "I guess we should sell off what we don't need. No point in hauling fish nets and such to the north. I reckon a good lure and a fishing pole would be all a man needs up there." He realized that he would soon have to go to the stage and face the pain of parting with the last of his father's belongings. Perhaps next weekend.

"Care for an iced tea?" Rose asked.

"Sounds fine," he replied.

Rose prepared a jug of tea and the two sat chatting about the move and looking out at the sea. They both avoided the emotion that accompanied the move, concentrating on the details of packing, selling, and cleaning. Soon the steaks were done and still Cadiz had not called or pulled up with Ellie Powers. A knot was forming in Rose's stomach with each minute that ticked past. Feigning the need for the bathroom, she slipped inside to use the phone. Ellie picked up on the second ring.

"Hello Ellie," said Rose with mixed feelings. She'd hoped Ellie was on the way with Cadiz. "Is Cadiz there?"

"Oh, hi Rose," said Ellie. "Hmmm, I don't think so, hang on," Rose could hear her call for Rod, then there was a pause. Ellie returned to the line, "Nope, haven't seen him all weekend."

Rose felt the blood rush to her face. "What?" She realized she said it a bit loud and tempered her voice. "Has Rod seen him?"

"Just a minute, I'll let you talk to him."

Rod came on, "Ya?"

"Hi Rod. I'm a little confused. I was under the impression Cadiz was spending the weekend wit' you. It's important that I find out where he is." Rose was trying to keep her voice even, fearful that Rod would withhold information to protect his pal.

"Ya, he was gonna stay here, but we kinda had a fight. He took off for home and I haven't seen him since." Rod's voice dragged like his tongue and brain had a lose connection.

"When was that?" Rose felt hot as the adrenaline surged through her.

"Friday, sometime after lunch," Rod answered.

Friday! Rose's thoughts were racing now. Where would he have gone? All possibilities escaped her. She turned to Rod.

"Where might he have gone?," she asked, desperate for a straw to grasp at. There was a pause that seemed endless. "Rod?" she asked.

"Well," he stammered. "It might be nothin', but he…" more pause, "…he was talking about getting on a bus and taking off. I thought it was just talk, prob'ly was." Sensing Rose's panic he quickly added, "I'll get my mom to drive me to Ernie's. Maybe they seen him."

"Thanks Rod, I'd appreciate that." Rose felt like she was on auto pilot. "Call me if you hear anything." She hung up and stood for a minute trying to formulate what she would say to John. He entered the kitchen with a platter of steak and foil packs in one hand and the empty iced tea jug in the other.

"You look a bit pale," he commented.

Heat had left Rose's face replaced by the cold fear of what had happened to her son. She slide into a chair and rested her head on her open palm. John set the food on the table and sat across from her.

"What is it?" he asked.

She could not meet his eyes and instead talked to the table top, "Rod hasn't seen Cadiz since Friday afternoon. I don't know where he is."

She could feel tears edging the rims of her eyes. Her throat tightened, like formulating the words of his disappearance was a poison. John sprang up, his chair scraping the floor like a scream. He paced the kitchen with fury, words echoing off the walls and windows.

"I'm sick to death of his shenanigans! When he shows up he'll be lucky to ever leave the yard. I told you it was ridiculous to let him loose all weekend!"

He raved for several long minutes, then announced he was going to look for him. Rose heard the start of an engine and then the truck tumbling out of the driveway. She pulled out the phone book and began making calls. Cadiz had so few friends, but she called anyone he had ever chummed with. When that revealed nothing she called her best friend Amy Watkins, wondering if Cadiz had been seen anywhere.

"Amy, dear, have you got a minute?" Rose asked.

"Jus' gittin' at the supper dishes," she replied. "What's up, luv?"

"I'm right beside meself wit' worry, Amy. Cadiz is missin' and I'm not sure where to begin lookin' for him." Rose felt relief flood through her, just in the act of confiding in her dearest friend. Tears threatened her eyes.

"Now what do you mean, missin'?" probed Amy.

Rose began with her call to Ellie, then back-tracked the conversations she had had earlier that day with Ms. Simmons and then Cadiz.

Amy did her best to placate her friend, promising to make some calls to neighbours and, reassuring Rose that Cadiz was probably just spending some time alone, as youngsters often needed to do. Rose hung up feeling much better. Tom and Amy had been neighbours for years. She and Amy had become afternoon confidants and the two couples had spent endless evenings of cards and easy conversation. Having had no children of their own, they had invested much time in Brian and Cadiz. Brian's death had been a great shock and they had shared in the family's deep grief. Rose would be forever grateful for their love and support. She trusted in it now.

Realizing she had been tying up the line, she called Rod. He too had not seen any sign of Cadiz, nor had Ernie. Rose made Rod walk her through all the events and conversations of Friday. When she hung up the phone, she could only reach one conclusion. Her son had run away.

She made a pot of tea and awaited John's return. As dusk settled like a bad omen, the truck pulled into the yard. She dashed to the door and her heart sank further to see only John stepping out of the vehicle. She told her husband of her conversation with Rod and they resolved to phone the RCMP.

As darkness approached, Cadiz packed up the meat. Not very dry, he would have to repeat the dehydrating process tomorrow.

"The seal's sealed," he said to Rod, slipping the plastic bag into the crevice and replacing the large stones. The bird hopped around awaiting a nibble. After the meat's recent sprint up his windpipe, Cadiz felt little desire to eat any. Instead he sucked on a Lifesavor while he replenished his water at the spring, then sought out fresh moss for his bed. All the while Rod circled above or did little dance steps nearby.

After several trips Cadiz had a cozy nest again, perhaps a little softer than the previous night. He resigned himself to whittling atop his rock to await the dark now that Rod had flown off to roost elsewhere. The sea rolled in a great calm rhythm, like smooth serpentine creatures moving northeast. The sun had long disappeared behind cloud and its last remaining light was slowly being snuffed by the horizon. Cadiz stared at the sea and sky willing them to materialize a boat or aircraft. The dark clouds withheld everything; stars, moon, rescue. The tide had changed its rhythm and Cadiz was unnerved by the gurgle and swish produced as the water swirled into empty spaces, pushing out the air. His imagination turned the sounds into footsteps, those of a corpse brought to life by a nosy boy's piece of driftwood. At times it sounded like voices, haunting him for disturbing the peace of the island.

Heart thumping, he quickly slid into the cave. To calm himself he pushed on the watch light. His shadow kept him company and he reached for the totems he had found that morning. He hoped they could distract him from the fear that was washing through him, the puppy in him cowering deep within. He stared hard at the tiny figures, trying to imagine the story they told. Fearing his watch battery would die, he turned it off and buried himself in the moss.

He spent a long sleepless night unable to close his eyes without seeing empty sockets staring back. He turned his attention to rescue. By now his parents were certain to have missed him. What were they doing? Had they sent a search party? He strained to hear above the rush of the tide. Several times he thought he heard his name drifting through the night. Once he had even braved the cold and dark to step outside. He looked out in all directions straining both ears and eyes for a sign. The sea was a moving, inky version of the black sky. He had imagined the voices and lost valuable body heat. It took a long time to heat his moss and little cave again. Cold climbed up and down his spine and sent waves along his limbs. He could not help but think of the dead man's winter coat. The thought of its warmth was fleeting, replaced by images of the snowmobiler, lumbering across the low tide and into the cave. Cadiz could imagine the wet eel grass dragging across his face, the bloated hands clutching at him, pulling him into the cold night and then into the even colder waters. The waves lapping at the shore became footsteps, the wind a raspy voice of death coming to claim him. His heart raced until it seemed it would burst out his temples and splatter the cave walls. He would have to rein his fear or daylight would be an eternity away.

He turned his thoughts from the oppressive darkness and ominous sounds and focused on his parents. Were they asleep, disregarding his disappearance? Were they searching themselves? Perhaps he would awaken to their voices. Mom would bring tea or hot chocolate, along with jam-jams. His mouth watered at the thought of the sweet sticky cookies. Dad would wrap him in a big blanket and build a fire. He would introduce them to the gull and show them his treasures. His father could alert the authorities that the missing snowmobiler had been found. Cadiz could see himself smiling out from the front page of the paper – the front page, not the obituaries, a newspaper, not a milk carton. He would have a great home-coming, with barbecued steaks and mom's great potato salad. There would be good music and friends he didn't even know cared. He imagined the comments about his bravery and how good it was to see him home. As the cave entrance began to lighten with the dawn, sleep finally claimed him. But sleep was not alone, it brought an ancient friend.

The RCMP officer had introduced herself, Meg Jefferies, and asked a barrage of questions. Rose felt like she was living a scene from an after school special. It was awkward having to tell the constable of Cadiz's recent instability and of their heartache and loss. The constable had assured them that Cadiz would likely show up, but that they would do their best to investigate. Rose had given the officer a recent school picture and was told that it would be faxed and emailed to other detachments. A member from the St. John's and Gander detachments would be sent, picture in hand, to ask questions at the airports. Gas station attendants would be quizzed to see if Cadiz was perhaps noticed hitching a ride. Rose was reassured by the fact that the constable had a young family. She would search as a cop, but also as a woman who knew the fears of a mother.

Amy had called back. She had no news of Cadiz having been seen anywhere, but her upbeat manner and sweet assurances had helped to slow the racing of Rose's heart. John had convinced her that they should try to get some sleep. She had gone through the rituals of bedtime: combing her hair, washing her face, and brushing her teeth. She slipped into the clean sheets, but as weary as she felt, she could not imagine herself falling asleep. A hundred horrible scenarios played out in her mind. After the loss of Brian she thought her life could not get any darker. Now she felt choked by a nightmare black as pitch. She heard the tap shut off in the bathroom and John appeared in the bedroom. He looked exhausted, dark circles aging his blue eyes. He climbed into bed and laid back, his hands latticed behind his head. They lay in silence for a while, each lost in dismal thoughts.

John replayed his search, re-driving various roads in his mind. He kept coming back to the stage. He had driven up and checked the door. The lock was intact, but he had circled the building looking for clues of Cadiz having been there. He'd found nothing. So why did he keep replaying the scene in his head? Was it because it was the only place he could think of to look? It was the most logical. More logical was the idea that his son had fled. He should never have dropped the idea of moving until Cadiz was finished school. The boy had run off disgusted with the thought of heading to Yellowknife. He was probably half way to Toronto by now. He would go to the bank in the morning to see if Cadiz had drained his meager young savings. That would be a sure sign that he had run away.

"Do you think you'll be gettin' any sleep? " asked Rose.

John rolled over to her and smiled. "Not too likely, is it?" he said.

Rose smiled back, "No, not very. Feel like a coffee?"

"Ya, how 'bout fillin' a thermos. I feel like takin' a drive."

John got up and started dressing. Rose went to the kitchen and soon the rich smell of coffee filled the house.

"We can take the cell phone in case the police find anything," John said, slipping the phone into his jacket. "I gave them the number."

They walked out into the night. The cloudy sky offered no light, and Rose could not help but feel trapped, as her waking nightmare continued. They drove through several familiar areas, looking intently, but not certain what they'd hoped to find. It seemed ludicrous to expect that Cadiz would materialize in their headlights, but they both carried the same silly hope. The radio filled the silence. VOCM, the Voice Of the Common Man, bellowed out its usual chorus of commercials, classics and complaints. The two were jolted from their pondering when Constable Jeffries came over the airways. She gave a brief description of their son and pleaded for information. When it was over John turned down the volume.

"That's bound to be helpful," he said, "not too many on this rock don't listen to the radio." He added, "Don't be frettin' my dear. The boy's just blown off steam, showin' us he's a man with a mind his own. We'll have him home in no time."

Rose nodded, but faced the darkened window. She did not want John to see her tear rimmed eyes. She was afraid that a show of affection from him might have her completely unglued. She rolled her eyes to absorb the tears before they streamed down her face.

A large amber light broke the night ahead and soon the hum of the crab plant's refrigeration could be heard. This time of year, the plants were open twenty-four hours. Seagulls roosted motionless on the red tin roof, and large transport tubs stood stacked, titan soldiers guarding the wharf. Several employees costumed in full rubber overhauls, milled outside, puffing on cigarettes and drinking from thermos lids or Styrofoam cups.

"What say we stop in for a chat," suggested John.

"Can't hurt," replied Rose, keeping it short so as not to betray the quaver in her voice. John cut he engine and the two approached the little gathering, who were clearly enjoying a coffee break.

"Good ev'n'en," John nodded. Rose smiled. They recognized almost everyone. Rose had worked with many and a few were from the same village. The crew raised their coffee in greeting or gave a nod. Ashlie Simon and Kayla Jesse stepped forward and gave Rose a brief hug. Both women had worked with Rose, and as mothers could imagine her grief.

"Don't worry, luv," Ashlie said quietly, "Cadiz is a good boy. He won't have gone far."

"Been listen'n ta the radio, eh?" John commented.

"Kids," said Kayla, as if that one word explained everything.

A rather large woman with big, netted hair and a dirty apron stepped forward. Rose didn't recognize her.

"I'd shake your hand," she said, "but I don't think you'd appreciate the crab stink on ya." She smiled. "The name's

Alana Tyler. Listen, it may be nutin', but a trucker was in today talkin about a young fella he give a ride to."

John and Rose both felt their spirits rise. She went on, "I didn't see the youngster, but the guy said he got directions from the lad. Could be your boy found a cheap ride to the mainland. Shipment was headed for Boston."

John jumped at the lead, "Could someone else have seen the b'y? Was he in the truck?"

"Don't know, he backed in and no one was outside. Wouldn't hurt to ask, but I'm the only one here was workin' Friday afternoon. It'll mean some calls."

John pulled out the cell phone and called Jefferies. As he passed on the information, Rose thanked Alana for her help. The crowd started to disperse, Kayla and Ashlie lagging behind to offer another supportive hug.

Back in the truck, John explained that the police would follow up as soon as possible. Jeffries was going to call the supervisor right away and obtain a list of people who would have been on Friday's afternoon shift. John recalled from his trucking days that the plants kept records of the trucks that came and went. Tracking the driver would take a little time, but it was inevitable that they would find him. Feeling that progress was being made, the two followed the headlights home and tried to get some rest.

11 ANCIENT FRIENDS

*C*adiz was surrounded by the night, but he could see the flicker of a light ahead. Its sunset colours told him it was fire. A boy stood on the pathway, beckoning him to follow. Longing for the warmth of fire and companionships he followed. He knew he should have been fearful and yet he felt only the longing. The boy looked to be about his own age, but his skin was dark. Black hair skirted black eyes. His clothes looked to be made of fur and hide. Cadiz picked up his pace to try to reach the boy, but he was always just out of reach. Suddenly the boy disappeared into a band of trees.

When Cadiz entered he was face to face with a fire encircled by a group of people. The trees hung 'round like a canopy, with just enough opening to chimney the fire. The group all sat, dressed in the same primitive wear. In the fire light he could see that their clothes were powdered in pink, their faces rubbed with terra cotta red. There were men and women, some with children wrapped in their laps. The boy sat next to a man of distinction, a man who had a face of creases that told of his wisdom. His long grey-pink hair set him apart from the others. He too wore the ancient clothing, but he also wore a necklace Cadiz recognized as a Beothuk relic. It held a great animal canine in its center. On either side hung three pendants that resembled highly decorated fork tines, some with three prongs, some with two. Cadiz's thoughts sidetracked briefly to Boyd's Cove Interpretive Centre. The guide had shown them pictures of such jewelry and artifacts of the pendants. The teeth, claws, and carved bones carried with them animal spirits used as charms for protection, strength and guidance. The red ochre rubbed into the shaman's pendants confirmed Cadiz's feeling that these were the Beothuk. Nearly every artifact and display in the Centre had been covered in the rusty-hued dust, denoting the Beothuk practice used to identify the tribe and to infuse all things with the life force represented by the ochre. How was it that he could be in their presence when that last of their nation had died over a century ago?

The elder reached out an open palm. Cadiz offered up his palm in return, and was shocked to note that three of the four totems he had found in the cave lay in his hand. The boy came and took the bear, the seal, and the wings, and placed the figures one at a time in the shaman's hand. Cadiz noted that the forth totem hung around the boy's neck. The elder sat and gestured for Cadiz and the young boy to each sit at his sides. He began to speak and all in the circle centered on his words. It was a language of long ago, but to his surprise, Cadiz understood it like it was his own.

"Young ones," he began, his voice rough as bark, "I want to ask you a riddle. It is of four creatures who all thought themselves invaluable and all thought themselves closest to the creator."

He held up the bear totem, then tossed it in the fire. Smoke rose from the flames, billowing and dancing until it became an ephemeral image of a great, upright bear. The shaman continued, "Bear thought himself fine, for he was resourceful and patient as a hunter, and had the strength to fall a tree."

The vein-sculpted hands held up the totem of the seal and again it disappeared into the flames. The smoke twisted into a seal reaching its nose high into the night. "Seal thought himself fine because he was gifted with speed and grace and a playful spirit. He believed bear should bow to him, because without him, bear would starve through the long winter."

The third totem, the bird, was fed to the fire and the smoke rose in a great puff, transformed into great outstretched wings, then disappeared into the night. "Gull though herself the finest. Her flight took her closest to the creator. Her feeding made her the friend to Mother Earth, eating what no one would have."

The boy pulled the totem from the sinew necklace around his neck and handed it to the elder. The elder tossed it into the fire and again the smoke contorted, this time into the image of a great stag Caribou. "Caribou was proud of his regal stance and strength of heart. He knew his value to the first peoples."

"So boy-with-antlers," the old one continued, his ancient eyes piercing into Cadiz's, "it is for you to decide – who among the three is most in the creator's favour?"

Boy with antlers? Was the shaman speaking to him or to the? What did this all mean? Cadiz wanted to speak, to ask questions, but he did not know the words. How was it that he understood them, but now sat mute. The answer to the riddle escaped him. He looked for the boy, but he could not find him. He swept his gaze around the circle. All eyes fixed on him, but the boy was gone. Cadiz felt fear creeping through him. Panic beat in his chest. The heat of the fire grew unbearable. He leapt from his seat.

The cold grey morning gripped him in icy disparity to the light and heat of his dream. He lay back and reflected on the images he had met in his sleep. Was his subconscious speaking to him or only his imagination? He opened his hand and saw the antler totem. He bolted up and began to search for the others. He found them hiding in the moss. Nothing supernatural. He must have dropped them as he was dreaming.

He rested for a while listening to the sounds of the island. He had grown accustomed to the steady beat of the waves, the hush of the wind, the crying of the gulls, but today the noise seemed harsher. The gulls were silent, but the wind had picked up and the waves beat angrily against the shore.

Cadiz's thoughts turned to the body on the neighbouring island. Perhaps it would be gone, washed out to sea. If he were going to find the courage to investigate, he would have to summon it by low tide. Even then he would likely get his feet wet in the crashing surf. He pondered the irony. He wanted to check the body in the event that it could help him create fire. He wanted fire worse than ever to fight back his nightly fear, which had been compounded by seeing the body. Was it worth going, returning to the ghoulish site?

As he debated his dilemma he set to work tidying his cave, setting the moss and garbage bag into place, and piling his little stack of dry wood and the skiver into the far corner. His mother would be proud of his efforts and he grinned thinking of how messy he kept his room at home. He couldn't wait to nestle into clean sheets after a hot shower and a bowl of his mother's hearty soup.

John pulled himself from bed and made his way to the bathroom. His stubbled face looked back at him, much too old to be his reflection. He could smell coffee and toast wafting up from the kitchen. He was hungry. In the stress of the previous night he and Rose had never gotten to the steaks. He cleaned up and went to meet his wife. He wondered how long she had been up or if she had slept much at all. They say opposites attract, but when it came to worrying he and Rose both seemed to do their fair share.

Rose was staring out the kitchen window, coffee in hand. He remembered the days when he used to sneak up behind her in a sweet embrace. Would she welcome that now or brush him away in her anxiety over Cadiz? The death and disharmony that had filled their lives had wedged between them, and he felt lost as to how to pull her back to him. Abandoning his thoughts of a hug, he poured a coffee and met her at the counter.

"Looks like some rain headed in," he said. "You get any sleep?"

"Some," she turned to him, and looking into her eyes, he knew a hug would be welcome. He took her coffee from her hand and set it with his on the counter. He took her in his arms and let her fall apart there. She cried quietly, her body trembling.

No words were spoken. There was no need.

Lost in their little reunion, they were both startled when the phone broke the silence. John answered and was greeted by Constable Jeffries.

"Good morning," she said. "We've been on the phone most of the night and early morning. Thought you might appreciate an update."

"Sure would," replied John. He smiled at his wife, noting the ridges of concern that had creased her brow.

Jeffries spelled out the events of the night. The police had located the supervisor at the plant. No one had witnessed the boy travelling in the truck, but the driver had been tracked. He had then been contacted by radio and called in. A police officer was currently sitting with him at a station in Boston. They would call with any developments. The good news was they would have more information soon. The bad news was the boy was no longer with the trucker, so they were still searching. The picture had raised no recollections from employees at the central airports or the bus stations. If Cadiz was on the run, he was most likely hitching it.

John thanked Jeffries and hung up. He refilled Rose's coffee and warmed up his own, then joined her at the table. He passed the news on to her trying to give it as positive a slant as possible.

"What do you think, John?" her eyes were pleading. "What's your feelin' on where our boy has gone?"

"He's okay Rose, I promise."

"You can't promise that!" Her voice had climbed. "First Brian and now to lose Cadiz. I can't stand it." Her hand came down hard on the table. She stood and walked to the window. "I don't know what I'll do wit'out my boys. I think I'd rather be dead."

The words stung John a little. Was he not worth anything to her? But he knew it was her grief talking. He followed her to the window and picked up the hug where they had left off. This time the phone stood silent. She sobbed for a time, wetting his shoulder. He fought the tears, trying to be strong, but he could not help letting a few escape down the lines that had recently etched his face.

Cadiz had breakfasted with Rod. The menu had consisted of a few strips of dried seal, a handful of last year's juniper berries, dry, stale and bitter, and a Lifesavor for dessert. He had made another attempt at fire with the flint and then the bow. His hands and shoulder ached, and the failure had left him feeling frustrated as usual. It had also raised a vortex of anxiety in his stomach, knowing he would have to return to the body. If there was any chance it would offer up fire, it was a place he had to go. The tide was ebbing and the little bridge exposed. Thick clouds added to the macabre feeling that gripped him. Wind and waves licked at him as he teetered and balanced his way across to the other island. His pace was understandably slow as he scanned the gloomy horizon. A few stray gulls swept passed the heavy sky. Rain was inevitable.

As he approached the scene of the body, he saw the heap of eel grass that shrouded the corpse. The snowsuit's bright orange trim that had first caught his eye seemed out of place in the dismal scene. He stopped to collect his courage. He had unconsciously been hoping the sea had claimed the body. Yet, he knew it might also offer up the warmth and security of fire. He took a few deep breaths and walked to the cold, tangled heap.

The eyeless face stared at him as it had in his dreams. He reached for the driftwood stick he had used and abandoned the day before. He tore the grass from around the midsection where he'd hoped to find the man's pockets. Bile threatened to rush up his esophagus and he swallowed hard. He fought to keep the panic from his breathing, taking air slow and deep into his lungs.

Sudden movement in his peripheral vision startled the air from him and he darted left. Rod had made a landing just over a meter away. He wandered about, oblivious to the horror he had joined. Cadiz steadied his nerves and dropped to his knees. With trembling hands he carefully pulled at the man's heavy coat. The head jiggled, thick with water. Cadiz kept his focus on the pockets and tried to block out everything else. His world seemed to slip into slow motion. He reached into the pocket, much like he would a spider infested hollow log. To both his disappointment and relief he found nothing. He stood and shook out the heebie-jeebies that had nestled into his bones. Then he repeated the process on the other side of the body. Again, the corpse offered up nothing but its empty sockets. He would have to dig inside the snowsuit and search the pants pockets.

He unzipped the snowsuit and pulled at the pocket to make room for his hand. The body shifted toward him and threatened to roll onto Cadiz's knees. Cadiz fell backward, heart ready to leap from his throat. The body stabilized and Cadiz leaned into it, eyes pinpointed on the pocket only. Once again he pulled it open, but this time more gently. He slipped three fingers into the pocket. Despite his fear, excitement seized him. He could feel cold, hard plastic! He reached further and gripped the object. He pulled it out and marvelled. A lighter!

He walked a few paces from the body and tried the flint. The mechanism was broken, but holding it up, he could see a fluid line dance inside. He prayed it was not water, but lighter fluid. Surely with all his efforts at fire, a little lighter fluid should push him to success!

Turning back to the body he was surprised to feel, not fear, but melancholy.

What if the body had been Brian's? Would he leave it there for the minks and the gulls? This body was that of a father, a husband, a son, and perhaps a brother. Cadiz decided that a burial might help to bring both he and the body a sense of peace. He heaped the eel grass back over the corpse and began combing the island for manageable pieces of rock. It was hard work, but with many trips he had made an impressive burial mound. He took a few moments, head bowed, then looked skyward and hoped that the man's soul had found a place much drier and happier than here. Rod glided past the grey sky and a great Osprey screeched its approval.

Cadiz decided it was time to return home, before the tide found its way too far up his little bridge. His pace quickened, provoked by the thought of the potential the lighter had held. He fought the urge to run across the bridge, reigning his enthusiasm with caution. Water reached for his shoes and the rocks teetered with the force of the waves.

In his concentration, he had not noted the great white mass at the northern tip of his little island. A massive polar bear had arrived from an ice floe and was shaking its heavy coat free of water. As Cadiz reached the safety of the shore, the immense bear picked up his scent and began to lumber toward him. Cadiz saw it and froze, then began to run toward the cave. His legs pumped madly and the uneven terrain threatened to send him sprawling forward. The grass and moss became a blur, his cave a dark haven that seemed an eternity away. He glanced back and saw that the distance between them had shrunken to only a few metres. He pushed harder toward the cave. He was almost there. He imagined hot breath on his neck and a great, clawed wrecking ball sweeping the air to lodge into his back.

He ducked into the tiny cavern and pressed hard against the south wall. The bear's head darted into the entrance puffing hot breath into the cave, then it pulled out, unable to enter. A huge paw raked the space just an arm's length from Cadiz's face and he pressed harder against the wall, wishing himself paper-thin. He had fought the sea, the rain, hunger and a corpse. Now he would die as a polar bear's midday snack!

John sat reading, awaiting a call from Jeffries. Over and over he tried to think of where his son might have gone. He and Rose had spent the morning phoning relatives, no matter how distant their blood or location: aunts in Toronto, an uncle in Calgary, cousins in Kingston, another uncle in Calais, Maine. As his mind darted from one idea to another, he couldn't help but come back to the stage. It seemed ridiculous, but he could not shake the feeling that he had missed something there. He put down the book and rested his eyes.

Suddenly, he saw it clearly. Brushing past the lower window he had peered at the inside counter. Was the dust there disturbed? Why hadn't it registered until now?! He wanted to leap from the chair, but he did not want to excite Rose if he was mistaken. He sauntered into the kitchen where she busied herself at the sink.

"I'm just steppin' out wit' me pipe Rose. I'll be right back."

Rose nodded in reply then returned to her thoughts and dishes.

At the back porch he found his jacket, keys still in the pocket, and stepped into a chill. The sky was ominous with thick clouds pressing down on the late morning. The air was still, building for the coming storm. Regardless of the coming weather, the air refreshed him and the walk would do him good.

Once at the stage he headed straight for the north side to check the window. He stood as tall as he could and peered into the interior. He was right! There was a clear path brushed across the width of the counter, a path about the width of a fifteen year old boy! John ran to the west side and fought to get the key in the lock. Its rusty works resisted, but it finally sprang open. John pushed open the door, and ran up the stairs calling for his son.

He was met by an eerie stillness. He walked through the little apartment, calling for Cadiz in each tiny room. Hope sprang within him as he noted the rumpled bedspread. He was sure Cadiz had been here, but where was he now? John paced the living room and noted the pictures and bric-a-brac. He had planned to be here cleaning next week. Now it seemed so unimportant, and almost a sacrilege to disturb his father's things.

He wandered down to the boathouse scanning his brain for ideas. When he got to the bottom of the stairs, he froze. Brian's kayak was missing! With all that that implied, John began to run home. His boy was at sea and he prayed that his youngest son had not met the same fate as his eldest!

12 DISCOVERY & DANGER

*J*ohn burst into the house at full speed and raced for the phone. He punched in the RCMP number and felt his heart thudding in his ears. Rose came in from the living room, panic settling into her marrow.

"What is it?" she begged.

"Brian's kayak's missin'. The fool boy's gone out ta sea." John replied as the third ring echoed through the receiver.

"RCMP, how can I help you?" a gruff male voice queried.

John asked for Jeffries and soon she was on the line. "John, I was just about to call you." Jeffries began. "I just got a call from an officer Deon Brown of the Boston Police. Apparently the trucker dropped a boy matching Cadiz description off near your place Friday afternoon. I know it doesn't make a lot of sense, but maybe he decided to run off afterward."

The words crowded impatiently in John's throat as he waited for her to finish. "It makes perfect sense," he said. "I've just been to the boathouse. Me oldest boy's kayak is missin'. Cadiz is at sea. I've no idea how long he's been out there. Could be since Friday, maybe only since Sunday or today. I'm headin' out in me boat. I'd appreciate it if you notified the Coas' Guard."

"Will do," Jeffries responded. "There are weather warnings, John. Make sure you've got company and keep an eye on the sky." Jeffries advised. "And stay close to the radio. The Coast Guard will have questions. Any idea where we're looking?"

"I've a pretty good guess. Rose will stay home in case Cadiz returns. She can give you the details." John looked at Rose as he spoke. Her look told him she was going to argue. He hung up and began to rummage through a drawer.

"You want me to just sit around an' wait while you go off ta sea? With the wind pickin' up and all that's happened to us?" Rose was incredulous.

"I need you here luv. I'm going to pick up Tom next door." He pulled a map from the drawer and spread it out on the counter. "I'll see if Amy will come and join you. When the Coas' Guard asks, tell them to look here."

He made a large ink circle on the map. "It's where Brian went down. It's only a guess. Cadiz might just be out pleasure cruisin', but if he's on a mission, this is where he'll go."

John grabbed a dark green slicker from the rack beside the door and headed out. Rose watched him head down the drive and turn towards Tom and Amy's. They were good neighbours and old friends. She hoped Amy would come. The wait would be nerve wrenching and she would appreciate the company. She would also need someone nearby when the authorities loaded her up with questions again. She stared hard out the kitchen window, watching

123

the wind swirl and the sky bruising to the deep grey of twilight, although it was only just after noon. The rains would be fierce. She wanted John safe with her, comforting her, and yet she was grateful that he was out searching for her baby boy. Why had life suddenly become so unpredictable and cruel?

She saw the flash of a yellow rain jacket. Amy bobbed up the driveway, jacket billowing above her head. It had started to rain just slightly and the wind was picking up speed. She went and opened the door to greet Amy.

"Land sakes, she's about to pour!" Amy said as she entered. She was a pretty woman, fairer and a few years younger than Rose, and time had been a little gentler on her features. Amy stashed her coat on a hook and wrapped Rose in a great hug.

"Don't fret dear," she said. "This will make a great story for your grandchildren someday!"

Rose forced a smile and went to fill the kettle for tea. She knew she would have to keep busy, burn her nervous energy before it paralyzed her or made her stark raving mad. The phone rang. It was Jeffries.

"Hello, Rose. Has John headed out yet?" she asked.

"Well, I don't think he's on the water, but he's on his way to the harbour," Rose replied.

"I'll reach him by radio," she went on. "The weather is turning pretty bad out there. The Coast Guard has advised the Auxiliary and small water craft to stay put. They've contacted Joint Rescue Control in Halifax, who will have Squadron 103 out of Gander do a sweep of the area by helicopter before the wind picks up too much more. Don't worry, Rose. They know what they're doing. If Cadiz is out there, they'll find him."

Rose's mind raced. *If* he's out there. What did Jeffries mean *if*. Of course he was out there! The helicopter would escort him home and this would all be a distant memory for the grandchildren. Right? She could think of no reply. She thanked Jeffries and headed for her coat.

"We should go tell the men the weather's too bad for the boats," Rose explained. "They won't have left yet." Amy understood her need to be doing something, so she too grabbed her coat and the two women headed for the wharf.

Captain Zach Cody of the Gander Airborne had just finished talking to Joint Rescue Control on the radio. He had the coordinates given to him via the missing boy's father. The Cormorant was fueled and ready. He and Lieutenant Tick Michaels could be airborne from Gander in less than ten minutes. Team leader Lukas Wagner, and his technicians Cassi Bernier and "Waves" Tooley of the 103rd Search and Rescue Unit were busily loading gear on to the chopper. The SARTECH team's bright orange coveralls stood in sharp contrast to the darkening sky. As always, the team geared themselves up for a happy ending. They hoped they would find the boy kayaking idly along, oblivious to the drama he had triggered.

The wind pushed at Cody and his copilot as they made their way to the helicopter. The five team members finished their checks and soon the hum of the engine fought to out-do the howls of the weather.

The land receded below them and soon they were

skimming along at five hundred feet. Cody and Michaels sat in the cockpit; Cody eyeing the sky, Michaels focused on the instrument panel. Wagner took the jump seat just ahead of the rear right door. From here he could see the landscape streak by and he would have a good jockeying point to man the door should they need to. Bernier and Tooley took the two rear jump seats, each allowing them a clear view through the bubble windows at starboard and port sides. As a team they worked together, each knowing their roles, but comfortable with any task they were assigned. They relaxed for the initial flight from Gander. The inland airbase meant it would take time to reach the east coast where they would begin their grid search pattern, beginning at the coordinates.

Cody hoped they would find the boy before this turned into a body search. As they approached the coast, Cody dropped altitude to 250 feet and their trained eyes swept the coastline for any debris. The water was getting choppy and a little craft would not last long. The kayak was wood, which was unfortunate. The brightly coloured fiberglass crafts were much easier to spot. The team could see a few fishing boats and pleasure crafts making their way to the little harbours that dotted the water's edge. As the Cormorant headed northeast and away from the mainland, the sea filled with little islands, like puzzle pieces cast away by a great god. Tooley's voice broke in on the headset.

"Check out the wildlife," he noted and pointed to a small island just ahead. The Crew saw a large polar bear poking at a rock formation below.

"Must have found himself some lunch," Cody smiled.

"Ever see such a crazy gull?" Wagner asked.

A small gull circled the bear. The bear would swipe at

it haphazardly then return to its interest in the cave. The gull was relentless. No other gulls dotted the angry sky.

"Winds picking up," Michaels advised. "We won't be up here long."

"We'll make a sweep a little further northeast, then turn south until we have to cut west back to Gander," said Cody. "The boy wouldn't have likely kayaked all the way to St. John's and I don't think that he'd head to Labrador," Cody grinned. He was only half serious. He'd hoped the boy's father was right. A narrow search would improve their chances. A wider search would widened the odds.

As Cadiz pressed hard against the cave wall an unfamiliar sound poked at his ears. Above the bear's raspy breath, and the crashing surf, was a distant clapping. He strained to make out the sound. A helicopter! He began to scream.

"Here! In here! Here I am!" He knew it was ridiculous to think that they would hear him, but he had to do something! Finally, rescue and he was cornered by five hundred kilos of fur and claws! The sound of the chopper became intense and then, just as quickly, the sound began to fade.

"Noooooo!" He screamed.

The distraction left him vulnerable for just a second. A great claw ripped through his jeans, close to his groin. He pulled back and began to flail about with his right hand, searching the cave for a weapon. He pulled up a piece of fir plank. To his pleasure and surprise it was the piece with the skiver attached. He began to lash out at the bear's paw. It reminded Cadiz of the make believe sword fights he and Brian had waged as kids.

He felt the plank make its mark. The paw disappeared and Cadiz held the plank in the dim light. It was bloodied. He had done some damage! He waited several minutes, expecting a paw or nose to fill the entrance. When it didn't he laid low to the cave floor and peered outside, careful to maintain a good distance from the opening. The rain had begun and the bear had gone over to easier fare. It was pushing away the boulders that protected his seal stash.

"Great," he said resting on the back wall, "now I'm back to slimy mussels."

He held the skivered plank in hand and decide to get comfortable and await the bear's next move. Perhaps if he was quiet, and the bear was full of seal it would wander on to something more interesting. He turned his attention to the slash above his left thigh. He could see no sign of blood and to his amazement he felt no pain. He felt his skin for a tear, but all was intact. His pocket hung from the hole like a cotton tongue and through a tear of its own Cadiz could see a coin glimmer in the faint light. He pulled it out through the ripped fabric and rolled it in his fingers. A heavy scratch defaced the queen. The coin had protected him from the bear's nasty claw. Opposite the queen he found the caribou holding its antlers in a proud stance. Cadiz recognized the same antlers from his dream. He pulled the totems from his rear pocket. He fingered the bear figurine, the bird, the seal, then the antlers. He realized that these animals had all figured into his castaway experience. *Coincidence?* He could not shake the feeling that something was unfolding, being shown to him.

Feeling more confident that the bear was preoccupied, at least for the time being, Cadiz watched the rain hop across the rock and let his mind ponder the totems. What about the Beothuk dream? A vision? He had read about many first nations that believed in visions. Had the burial site, if that's indeed what it was, triggered something deep within him? What about the shaman's question. Cadiz reflected on it. What was closer to the creator? The bear? The bird? The seal? The caribou? It seemed clear to Cadiz that the bird was of little significance. After all, gulls were a nuisance most of the time. Seals were pretty and useful, but they didn't inspire the respect of a fierce bear. He remembered that a skinned bear was said to look very human. He resolved that the bear must be closer to the Creator. After all it was stronger and further up the food chain.

His thoughts turned to the helicopter. Would it return? Was it a rescue chopper or was it just a coincidence? He had to believe his parents would be searching for him. It was Monday afternoon. Surely they had noticed him missing last night. It was just a matter of time. He remembered the lighter fluid in his pocket. Perhaps he would be able to make a signal fire. He would have to wait out the bear and the rain, but then he would get to work. The helicopter would touch down and find him casually feasting on steamed mussels and hot Labrador Tea. He transferred his knife and coin to his back pocket along with the four totems. He helped himself to a Lifesavor before tucking them into the opposite rear pocket.

"I could use a little saving," he whispered, and popped it into his mouth. He risked a closer peek out the cave door.

He could see the bear making its way to the beach. The rain was now coming in great sheets. He would have to work quickly to collect a few more planks before they were too water logged to be useful. He was thankful that he had been wise enough to store a few in the cave on the first night. They would make excellent kindling. When he saw the bear crossing the channel to the neighbouring isle, he crouched low and went to collect the planks. He pulled several from the bottom of the pile and raced back to the cave. In the few moments he had exposed himself to the rain it had soaked him to the skin. The wind was pelting it down like small stones. Tiny rivers raced down from his hair and made their way across his face and down his back. He huddled into his moss nest and watched the silver sheets sweep across his little island. He had kindling, he had fuel, but it would do him little good. Starting a fire in his cave would only smoke him out into the cold evening. He peeled his sweatshirt from his body, reversed his seal vest and put in on. He would cuddle in and hope the rain would break long enough for him to build a signal fire.

It would be another night of splintered dreams. A caribou chased him through thick forest landscapes. A gull tried to peck at him as he fled from an angry bear. A seal looked helplessly up at him, its blood soaking into his shoes. The bear, the gull, the caribou and the seal fought and tore at something he could not identify, seeming to compete for some prize. The Beothuk boy tried to tell him something, but he could not hear it above the pelting rain. An ancient face smiled and faded…

13   RESCUE

*C*adiz awoke to a sound that had become unfamiliar –
stillness. The surf still pounded on his little isle, but the
hammering of the rain that had turned his shelter into the
inside of a snare drum had stopped. The rock lay in relative
quiet. He checked his watch; 4:35 a.m. Cadiz rose stiffly
from his clump of moss, took a deep breath of rain soaked air,
and peered out into the night. The cloud cover offered no
moonlight and the landscape melded with the sea. He would
have to venture out a ways to find out if his bear visitor was
still vacationing on his isle. He poked his head out and
waited for a massive claw. Instead, he was prickled by the
chill that crept across his flesh. He pulled a few dry planks
from inside and began to tear them into thin strips with his
knife. Soon a small, spaghetti-like heap formed between
his knees. He pulled his bow-lighter from within the cave
and then pulled the lighter from his pocket.

"Its now or never," he whispered, and felt a great weight
begin to lay across his chest. The meager stash of lighter
fluid would offer up only one chance. If he failed, he would

forgo hot food, warmth, a rescue fire, and quite possibly, his hope for survival. Cadiz read the inscription on the blade – *Let your own hand whittle your destiny.* Then he looked to the charcoal sky.

"I'm whittling Granddad. I appreciate the calm, and the lighter fluid. Would I be pushin' my luck to ask you and Brian for a spark?" He tilted his head with a wink, then set to work.

He set the lighter atop a small pile of dried moss and let down with a large stone. The lighter smashed apart and the liquid hope crept slowly across the moss. Cadiz placed his small heap of kindling atop the moss then placed the stick at its centre. Holding the bow steady, he began to move the bow back and forth. It slipped, threatening to toss his pile like a salad. Cadiz breathed deeply, set his jaw, and began again. This time he fell into a steady rhythm. With each saw of his hand, he visualized fire licking up from the pile. After several endless moments Cadiz smelled the lighter fluid begin to heat. From the darkness, below the kindling, a tiny flame flickered and with it Cadiz's belief that life was beautiful. The puppy in him wanted to jump about, to wag a wild tail and nip at the moon. Instead Cadiz inhaled slowly, nestled his face closer to the flame and began to blow gently. He would have to be patient, and nurture the flame into something substantial. Soon the flames were licking at his thin strips of wood, eating them hungrily. He split a few planks in half length-wise and set them carefully on top. These too quickly began to alight and Cadiz knew he could celebrate.

He leapt in the air and twirled skyward laughing. Tears sprang to his eyes and he shouted to the dark sky, "Here I am! Here I am! Thank you Brian! Thank you Granddad! They'll find me now!"

With a great "Whoop!" he made his way to the wet stack of planks and pulled some from the bottom. They were damp, but they would burn! Once Cadiz had nurtured his little fire to its independent adolescence, he carefully made his way to the spring to collect tea leaves and water.

While he sopped water into the bottle the sky faded from black ink to dull pewter. With the coming of light Cadiz planned to collect mussels to steam for his breakfast. He pocketed a handful of Labrador Tea leaves and returned to his fire which danced in the distance like a warm and welcomed friend. He added a few more planks to the fire which smoked and sputtered from the damp. When the flames had rested a little, Cadiz stirred a place in the fire to expose a nest of embers. There he placed his half filled bottle and watched the magic his Granddad had showed him possible. The plastic bottle shrank a little and its clear surface clouded to a smoky grey. Soon the water began to bubble up to the rim, but the plastic held its shape. Using his glove, Cadiz pulled the bottle from the embers and tossed in the tea leaves. He placed the funnel atop and let it steep. It smelled musky and delicious. To spoil himself, Cadiz added a Lifesavor and swirled it around the cup to let its sweetness mingle with the leaves. His stomach contracted and his mouth filled with saliva. "High tea," he said with a grin and stuck out his pinky in mock snobbery. Before it could cool to anything reasonable, Cadiz had to relish a sip. It burned a little, but the rum and butter tea concoction was music to his tongue. He took a second sip and let it swirl around his mouth, coating it and conjuring memories of ice cream, cheesecake, milkshakes, all things sweet and wonderful.

When he downed the last of his tea, it was far from full sunrise, but the ashen light was plenty bright for a skilled beachcomber to harvest a meal. The tide was high and rising, forcing Cadiz to reach long and deep for the mussels. He lay flat along the shoreline, where he had first arrived on the isle. Its steep and rocky edge would be bountiful. He plunged his arm into the frigid water. His fingers began to numb and he had to be careful not to do damage to his slowly healing fingertips. With the missing nails, they were vulnerable. As he ripped a handful of small mussels loose from the rock, his one finger scrapped hard against the granite. Tears sprang to his eyes. "Patience ol' boy," he whispered, then tried again. It took almost ten minutes crawling on his belly, feeling gingerly along the rocky ledge, but Cadiz had made himself a small pile of about twenty mussels. They were high water mussels, tiny but tender. He gathered them into a pouch made by folding his sweatshirt out and upward, then walked back to his fire. After the cool rock on his belly and the icy water up to his underarm, the warmth of the fire was spectacular. Cadiz sat for a minute simply enjoying its heat. The sky was fading yet again, molting its pewter finish for shades of pink and silver. Rod returned with the dawn, but kept his distance from the alien flames. Cadiz threw a couple more planks on the fire and realized he would have to become more frugal with them. The present fire would have to be enough to prepare his breakfast, then he would have to nurture it just enough to keep it alive throughout the day. Fire would be more valuable to him in the cold evenings and he had no idea how many days it would have to last. He would have to return to the neighbouring isle at low tide to collect what driftwood and debris he could find.

He tossed the mussels directly on the fire and settled in to enjoy the heat and watch them cook. Soon they began to spit and open, indicating they were ready to devour. Cadiz's mouth watered and he could not help but remember the taste of warm butter and vinegar, the way his mother had always served them. He used the old glove to poke and flip them free of the hot ashes, so that they could cool a little. When they seemed safe to touch, Cadiz lifted one from the pile and pulled it apart. The inside was still steaming, but Cadiz could not wait. His belly growled its desire and he tugged at the rubbery morsel with teeth and tongue. It lacked the rich taste of butter, but it was a far sweeter bite than the fishy slime he had had to choke down just days before.

The thought crept across Cadiz's mind, *just days before.* It was only Tuesday morning. He had crashed here only four nights ago and yet it seemed he had been here a lifetime. It seemed a decade since he had seen his parents, a decade since he had enjoyed the lather of a soapy shower, a decade since he had shared laughter with a friend. A *friend*, he wondered how Rod was doing. Rod would have had to go to school to face Clark and his wrath, Ms. Simmons and her well-meaning probing, the many questions the kids would have about his disappearance. Would they care? Would Rod care? Surely they must be searching for him. He remembered his last real conversation with Rod, sitting on the shore, discussing the thrill and impossibility of running away. Is that what they would assume? That he had run off? Would anyone bother to run after him?

Cadiz felt the wild dog awaken in him. He placated it with a mussel, then another. It was so much easier to ease the body than the mind. Cadiz finished the mussels, then pushed his little fire into a tight pile to conserve its heat and fuel. He stared at its glowing embers and felt the heat of pride swell in his chest. He had done it! Here he sat, fed, watered and warm. He had survived a crash, a dead body and a bear. He had lived through nightmares and rain and doubt. Whatever the days ahead brought, he could draw on these small victories to soothe him. These thoughts washed over him, back and forth with the waves that lapped with the rising tide and the lightening sky, so that they lulled him almost into sleep.

Suddenly the spell was broken by a second rhythm, one less melodic, more sharp and ever increasing. It took Cadiz a few seconds before the realization anchored in his head. It was the sound of a helicopter!

Cadiz ran to his meager pile of wood and threw three planks on the fire. He blew it back to a blaze and searched the sky for a visual on the chopper. It broke into view like a wild mirage and Cadiz began to jump and wave his arms. It was approaching from the south end and Cadiz began to run toward it, all the while his arms fanning the air like a drunken traffic cop. With the adrenaline rush and the rocky terrain, Cadiz lost his stride, stumbling forward, the ground rushed up at him. An angry rock caught his temple and his world went black.

Search and Rescue Unit 103 was ready at first light. They would cover the same grid pattern as they day before, then broaden their search in an ever increasing circle. Captain

Cody and Lieutenant Michaels did their checks while the SARTECH trio, having finished theirs, strapped in for what promised to be a smooth ride. The wind and rain from the previous night had calmed and the skies, though cloudy, offered little threat.

The helicopter lifted from the Gander air base, hovered slightly southward, then circled and shot eastward toward the coast. Once at the water's edge, their eyes immediately scoured the shore, and became keener as they entered the grid pattern zone. White foam bubbled along the jagged slabs of rock that spattered the sea. Uneven blotches of green broke up the pattern of the terrain and water; evergreens struggling for their right to remain. A moose made a thin trail near a pond edge and a variety of birds peppered the islands. Small communities tried desperately to civilize the feral landscape, but to no avail.

"We're coming up on the boy's village now," said Cody into his headset.

The team nodded and their posture indicated it was time to sharpen their focus that much more. Within minutes they were in the zone, the area the boy's father had indicated the boy was likely to have travelled. Weather reports for the days the boy was likely to have paddled out indicated that their best bet for finding him, or wreckage from his craft, would be north of his village.

"Smoke at two o'clock," Wagner said as he pointed off his right cheek.

Cody put slight pressure on his right foot and the chopper tilted right. A thin wisp of smoke could be seen in the distance.

"Any word from the Coast Guard about activity in this area?" asked Tooley.

"Nope. Hopefully we've found our boy." Michaels smiled, "Could it be that easy?"

The crew smirked in unison. Some days were easy, some days broke your heart.

"Isn't this the site of the bear with the looney gull side-kick?" asked Bernier. "I do believe it is," answered Wagner.

As the Cormorant came closer, a human figure could be seen running. Suddenly, the figure dropped to the ground.

"What the…?" Cody began.

The SRU leader finished, "We got ourselves a fallen one, gang. Nothing's ever easy is it?" Wagner sighed into his headset. This happened. Survivors were sometimes overcome with the adrenaline rush of rescue, some fainted from dehydration. There were many reasons to have to reach down to scoop up the victims.

"The terrain's too uneven." Wagner went on, "Best plan on a cable pick up. Cass, Waves, you two are going down to bring our boy home. Cass, you'll go first."

Waves gave him a wink and he and Cass began to suit up for a cable rescue. Waves would steady the cables while Cass went down with the medic pack to assess the boy's condition. Waves would follow her down to steady the cables for her assent with the boy, while Wagner prepared the stretcher and supplies on board. Cody focused on maneuvering his aircraft for his SARTECH pendulums, while Michaels radioed in their coordinates keeping a close eye on his instruments and the sky. They were a well-oiled machine and it would not take long to have this boy back in the arms of his family.

14 HOMEWARD

*C*adiz looked through the darkness to a distant flickering light. He recognized the path – a trail that led to the Beothuk of his dreams. He rose slowly and walked with leaden legs, his head trying to piece together his disjointed world. The circle emerged with its fire at the center. The tribe all looked to the shaman who sat cross-legged, a bowl in one hand, his other hand smeared red powder on a young face.

Cadiz recalled the spring ochring ceremony he had seen enacted at the Beothuk visitor center in Boyd's Cove. These people were preparing to part company, branching into their smaller satellite groups for the bountiful summer. Cadiz slipped into the circle and was about to sit when the creased shaman summoned him to sit closer. The tribe sat quietly, their hair, skin and furs freshly dusted in cinnamon pink. Cadiz stepped cautiously around the fire and sat cross legged next to the old stranger, who seemed, somehow, like family.

"You have come for the protection of the red dust…"

Cadiz was uncertain whether the ancient leader was

asking him a question or declaring a truth. He nodded slightly, afraid to contradict and thereby offend the elder. The now familiar boy smiled at Cadiz from the elder's other side.

"Have you solved the riddle?" the elder asked.

Cadiz shook his head no, then dropped his gaze, feeling small and ashamed. The elder put out his hand, palm upward. Cadiz mirrored him and, once again, saw three of the four totems laying in his hand. The elder took the bear, and as before, tossed it into the fire. Again the smoke swirled into a great dancing bear. As it twirled skyward, Cadiz's breath hitched in his chest. The image briefly contorted and Cadiz saw clearly the smiling specter of his granddad.

"Wisdom, strength and patience," the elder spoke, "these are the gifts of the bear." Cadiz looked to him, then back to the fire. The smoke and its haunting image of Granddad were gone.

The old one reached for the seal totem and pitched it into the flames. Cadiz's eyes were focused hard on the smoke billowing above the flames. Again it swirled and transformed into the image of a seal. As it moved skyward it stretched out into a clear, but wispy version of Brian. He smiled down on Cadiz, but Cadiz could not return his grin. Instead great tears filled his eyes. He blinked them away, trying to hold on to the vision of his big brother. As quickly as it formed, it disappeared. The elder's voice broke through the pain in Cadiz's chest.

"Grace, agility and a playful spirit, these are the gifts of the seal." As he finished speaking, he reached for the third totem, the wings. Once again, he tossed it into the fire. The smoke rose into two wings, opening over the flames.

Cadiz was riveted to them, awaiting the next image. His eyes widened as each wing took on a separate form. To the right was his mother, to the left his father.

The old one spoke again, "These are the wings of the gull."

The gull? thought Cadiz. But he had named his gull Rod, thinking it silly, even stupid.

The old one went on, "The gull is the companion of the sea. Her cry breaks the loneliness, her wings protect her young. These wings move her forward through each day, each season. These are her gifts."

Cadiz felt both awe and shame tear at his chest. He had treated his parents so badly. He had shut them out and yet they were as important to him as his Granddad, as his brother. They were more important, because they were there for him.

The Beothuk boy rose and bowed to face the shaman who took something from around the boy's neck. As the boy turned back to his seat, the fire light caught the totem that hung from the shaman's hands. Cadiz recognized it as the forth totem he had found, the antlers. The elder motioned him to stand and Cadiz took the place the boy had stood in only moments before. The elder pressed down on his shoulders and Cadiz knelt before him. The old one placed the totem around Cadiz's neck and then began to ochre the lines along Cadiz's face, beginning at his forehead, following the bridge of his nose, then sweeping outward across his cheeks and down his chin. He then made several sweeps from the crown of Cadiz's head down to his hairline and as he did so, he spoke.

"The caribou totem you share with my grandson. For my people this animal holds a great place. It is majestic in its walk and strong in its fight. It is much necessary to the survival of our people. The creator blesses each animal with gifts, gifts to be sacrificed and shared for all. Each one shared becomes part of the other in the great and intricate web of creation."

When the old one finished tracing ochre along Cadiz's arms and chest, he took Cadiz's face in his hands. "Find your place in the web, boy-with-antlers. Do not underestimate your place in creation. Seek out this place, make it your own, nest there and then share it with others. All are important to hold the web together and to add to its beauty."

He let go and Cadiz felt himself begin to rise. He began to swirl skyward, above the flames. As he looked down on the fire and faces below, he began to wonder if he was dying. Was he going to meet Granddad and Brian? Was this what death was like- warm and surreal and so peaceful? He was excited, but also reluctant. He had so much to do, so much to live for. Still, he spun quietly skyward. Why would the elder reveal these things to him, if it were too late. He looked up, expecting to see his brother reaching out to him, his granddad summoning him with outstretched arms. Instead he saw bright orange-red metal.

A great noise filled Cadiz's ears and he could see the underside of a huge helicopter. A strange face peered at him from above. He looked down again, but this time it was not the Beothuk circle he saw, but his little isle. It looked small and from its centre, atop his cave, his Beothuk friend waved to him. Behind the boy was the faint silhouette of a great caribou. Cadiz waved to them and watched as they faded, burned away like fog in sunlight. The island receded beneath him and suddenly he was being pulled inside the chopper. A great harness encompassed his torso and bit at his groin and he realized he'd been strapped to a woman in bright orange coveralls. A mustached man with greying temples was undoing the many straps that held he and the woman as one.

The man slid a cuff up onto his arm and began to take his blood pressure. "Hi, I'm Lukas," he said, holding out a handshake. "You're going to be okay now, son."

Cadiz took his hand and shook as firmly as his weak body would allow. Wagner helped Cadiz onto a stretcher, anchored to the wall opposite the large door they had used to enter the craft. The woman removed her helmet revealing pretty chestnut hair plaited back over kind hazel eyes. Lukas continued to inspect Cadiz, shining a small instrument into his eyes and ears. Another man, tall and broad entered the chopper. He removed his helmet and smiled wide, "I'm Lindy, but me friends calls me Waves."

"Good to meet you," Cadiz smiled. They all grinned at the deeper meaning that the little phrase held.

Cadiz sat on a stretcher watching the sea and islands moving by in a blur below them. He thought he saw a small seagull tailing them far below. The bird triggered a memory and Cadiz reached into his back pockets for his totems. Instead he pulled out his knife, a scratched quarter and the last of his Lifesavors. Three candies remained. He offered them to his rescuers, who each accepted the sticky little gift with a smile.

"Trade you" said the woman as she handed him a cup. "My name's Cassi."

Cadiz took a small swallow. *Mmmm*. Sweet juice danced over his tongue. He downed the rest of the drink, then laid back and closed his eyes. There were no totems in his pocket. Had he left them behind? Had they ever been there? Cassi tucked a blanket around him and smoothed his hair back, like his mother had when he was a child. He held his knife and the quarter close to his chest and let his thoughts trail off. Soon he was in a deep sleep, uninterrupted by cold, nightmares or Beothuk visions.

EPILOGUE

 he crisp smell of fresh sheets filled Cadiz's nostrils. He could feel a soft mattress beneath him. He hesitated before opening his eyes. Was it all a dream – the rock, the cold, the haunting darkness? Where was he? His Granddad's loft? His own warm bed? He lifted heavy lids and let them flutter as the warm sunlight filtered in through an undressed window and his lenses adjusted. He was stricken with the starkness of his surroundings. Bright white walls stood out from behind a small TV screen. A large door stood a quarter way open and its huge chrome handle screamed "institution." He looked over his shoulder and confirmed his suspicions when he saw the plastic intravenous tubing running from his left arm up into a bag of clear liquid. He was in the hospital.

A plethora of images swirled in his head. He remembered his island: his cave, his bird, his pocketknife. He remembered his vision; the elder, boy and the totems. He remembered his chopper ride home and the last of his Lifesavors. He had a vague idea of his mom and dad huddled over a gurney, as he was whisked on rickety wheels from the chopper and into an ambulance.

He sat up slowly, his head spinning at first, then settling to a dull thumping. He reached for a plastic cup on the bedside table and took a sip from the straw. Cool, clean water brought his dry mouth to life. He smiled at how easy it was to simply reach for water. He leaned back against the soft, fresh pillow and closed his eyes. He let the memories of his experience swirl in his head and watched as they slipped into place like the pieces of an intricate puzzle...

The totems had been no coincidence. He had shared the burial site of a Beothuk boy of long ago. He wondered at what had happened to the boy, but that vision had not been revealed to him. Instead the boy had brought him to the elder, a man of wisdom who helped him see through the confusion and despair to the lesson's life was offering him. What had he learned? His brother, agile and full-spirited, had taught him to embrace life, to see its many pleasures and great joys. He had almost let go of that in his grief. He would hold that lesson close to him from now on. His parents, always there to lead and to embrace him, had taught him to temper his spirit for the many seasons life would offer, to ride the winds of change and to nestle close to home when things got harsh. In his grief, he had pushed them away, but he would reach for them, as he should have from the beginning. Granddad, strong and patient, had pointed him to his totem. Granddad had taught him to search not only the land and sky, but his heart, which would reveal a destiny to be carved out. He would find his scratched quarter, have it drilled to hang on a chain from his neck. He learned that he was necessary and that he had an important role to play. He wondered what that role would be, but his thoughts began to scatter with the thumping that filled his skull.

He opened his eyes and felt his head. A bandage hid whatever damage had been done to his left temple. Some of his fingers had been bandaged too. He swung his legs out from the sheets and blankets and noted the draft wafting through the back of his hospital gown. *Who invented these dignity-thieving pajamas anyway?* He smiled, and the smile felt so good. He stood cautiously on the cold tiles, pulled the IV pole closer and then wheeled it forward to make his way to the bathroom. He smiled again at the luxury and uncommon beauty of the porcelain toilet shining in the well-lit bathroom.

Having completed his business, he stood washing his hands. He let the warm water wash over them, then splashed the liquid comfort over his face. He looked in the mirror and saw a tired, but happy face. Bringing his hand to his cheek, he realized how many faces he saw there. A mirror behind him was reflecting his image again and again and again. In each image he could see his father's determined jaw, his mother's firm but gentle hand, his granddad's knowing eyes, his brother's impish grin. In each reflection, like a portal back through time, he had brought each generation forward. His average face carried the genes and the stories of the ages and suddenly he was looking at something glorious, something so beyond and above average, something to be revered, like an ancient volume. At that moment Cadiz realized that no matter where life took him – Yellowknife, a lonely isle, or a port – in Spain, he would whittle his own destiny. It would be a destiny of significance, not because of who he would become, but because of who he was. He was Cadiz; a boy, a branch whittled from a family tree of great strength, anchored with deep roots. He breathed deeply, inhaling the importance of the moment, then dried his face and pulled his IV pole into the open room.

As he stepped from the bathroom, the door to his room swung open and in walked his mom and dad. His mother took him in her arms and squeezed so tightly he though he might break in half. His father embraced them both in a great bear-hug and tussled Cadiz's hair as he had done years before. Cadiz felt whole in their hugs – hugs so big they could chase away cold, fear, loneliness, even a wild dog.

"I love you, Mom," he said with pride. "You too, Dad."

"We love you," they said in unison.

Outside the hospital window a one-eyed gull took flight toward a calm sea and into a clear open sky.